Now You Wanna Come Back

Anna Black

www.delphinepublications.com

Published by. Delphine Publications, LLC.

© 2010

ISBN-13- 978-0-9821455-5-5

Second Edition

First Printing, November 2010

Delphine Publications focuses on bringing a reality check to the genre urban literature. All stories are a work of fiction from the authors and are not meant to depict, portray, or represent any particular person. Names, characters, places, and incidents are either the product of the author's imagination or are used fictitiously, and any resemblances to an actual person living or dead are entirely coincidental.

Published and printed in the
United States of America

www.delphinepublications.com

Also By Anna Black

Luck of the Draw

Who Do I Run To?

Coming Soon

Now You Wanna Come Back Too

Dedication

This book is dedicated to my readers, whom I really appreciate. I do what I do for the sake of making people laugh, cry, smile and reflect. I really hope that all of my readers enjoy this story and will be anxious for my stories to come. Thank you all for your support and be on the watch for my next book – trust, it will be worth reading.

Enjoy!

Acknowledgments

Oh my God, I did it! Thank you Lord, thank you Father. Thanks to my parents, Lue and Marvin Sr., for coming together and making wonderful me, (yeah). To my family and close girl friends, (y'all know who you are), thanks for your support and encouragement to keep on going. A special thanks to my brother Vi, who told me, *"Keep writing girl, that's what you were born to do,"* when I just wanted to say forget it. Thanks so much to Ghostwriter Extraordinaire (GWE) for my book trailer; it is awesome, thanks so much. I am so, so grateful to God for allowing this because it was a long time to come, but I did accomplish my dream of publishing a book; just hoping he'll allow this again because I have more to deliver. I would also like to give a huge special thanks to my husband, Chris for putting up with my late nights at the computer and my time not spent because I had to work on one of my books. Thank you Tyra, my baby girl for understanding when mommy needed quiet so I could concentrate. My Godson Tyrik, just for being my baby and to my girls, Chanda, Dominique, Tara, Elsie, Gail, Latonya, Dee-Dee, Yoruba, Joyce, Monique, Athena, Legazy and my sister Tandra (Nina). I love you all; each and every one of you has touched my life in some way over the years, so thanks guys. Lastly to my girl, Sha-Nelle, who told me to publish this book first and I hope you were right girl - lol. Lastly - huge thanks to my publishing company Delphine Publications for having me and making me a part of this literary family. Lastly to Davida Baldwin, truly a talented sister for giving me such a beautiful cover for my first published novel.

I am grateful to God for so many blessings. To have a creative mind is a gift and I thank Him. To allow my stories to be enjoyed by others is also a blessing. Thank you my readers, for giving **Now You Wanna Come Back** a chance to be read by you.

Just always remember to *"Be You, Do You, & Love You."*
Happy Reading!!!

Now You

Wanna Come

Back

I

I know you see this rock on my finger, Leila thought to herself as she handed her customer his bank card. He had come into her bookstore about an hour ago to purchase some literature on healthy eating. Yes, he was fine and had a killer body, but she was in no mood to deal with his arrogant ass.

He walked in the store confidently, because he was drop-dead gorgeous, but as soon as he opened his mouth he was drop-dead asshole. He went on and on about himself and how he was this well-known personal trainer in the Chicago area. Of course Leila, a size sixteen mother of an adorable three-month-old little girl, did not have any knowledge of whom or what he was, nor did she care. Although he meant no harm and was not the egotistical asshole she perceived him to be, the sound of his confident voice made insecure Leila want to scream.

She showed him the health items that she had in stock and made a huge mistake by telling Mr. Physical to let her know if he needed any help. She went back to her stool behind the counter and opened the novel that she was reading by Anna Black called *Who Do I Run To,* when he asked his first question. She got up, walked over and grabbed the book that he asked her about - that sat right in front of his face - and handed it to him.

'If it hadda been a crocodile, he'da been eaten, that's for sure,' she said to herself as she walked away. She headed back toward the counter and question number two came, which caused her to stop in her tracks. She turned her attention back to him and satisfied him with an answer and by question number fifteen, she referred him to the Internet, which was set up in a nice and quiet corner of her store to allow customers to look up material on their own.

That computer and Internet set up was a lifesaver for her on the days she worked by herself and *'days like this when annoying ass customers won't leave you the hell alone,'* were her thoughts as she sat back behind the counter. The store was empty for a Saturday and she took advantage of it by catching up on some of her reading. It was usually a madhouse, but since the day was slow, she sent her other staff home.

Once she put her nose back into her book, she was praying he would get what he needed and bounce because it was getting good and she didn't want to stop reading. He finally made his way to the counter with only one book to purchase, after all that.

"Will this be all?" Leila asked him when he handed over his bank card.

"Yes and your number would be nice?" he said flashing his gorgeous smile and perfect white teeth.

"Ump ump," she said, clearing her throat, handing him his card and pointing out the fact she was wearing a ring. Not just a ring, but a gorgeous three-karat, princess cut diamond ring.

"Aw my bad, I didn't realize that was a wedding ring," he said, as if he were implying her stones wasn't all that.

"Yes it is," she said sharply.

"Oh excuse me, I do apologize Miss Lady."

"It's okay. You have a nice day," she told him and handed him his bag. He stood there for a moment like he was waiting for something more.

"Hey Leila," he said reading from her nametag. "My name is Rayshon Johnson, but mostly everyone calls me Ray. Here is my card. If you are ever in need of a physical fitness trainer hit me up. I'll give you a good deal," he said, giving her one of his cards. She took it, looked at it quickly and put it with a stack of business cards that had been left by other customers who had made purchases at her store and like those cards she would never call him either.

"Well Rayshon I thank you for your offer, but as you can see, I don't do gyms, nor do I do physical trainers. Have a nice day," she said, giving him a wink.

"Oh, so you think only fit people have trainers?"

"Are you implying I'm not fit?" she asked with much attitude.

"No, no I'm not, you are a thick sista and that's fine. You look damn good and I'm not trying to make you skinny; just wanna help you to be healthy. So please don't take it offensively, because I personally prefer a thick sista, but at the same time, I want my woman eating right and putting in some type of cardio. Even if it's only thirty minutes a day, it all helps for a healthier heart," he said, sounding caring, not like the '*I'm too sexy for my shirt,*' asshole that he came into the store as.

"Well Rayshon thanks, but I'm good. If ever a day my husband and I wanna hire a personal trainer, you'll be the first one we call," she said, changing his bright smile to a look of defeat. He eased back from the counter he was leaning on and backed up a bit.

"Well alright Ms. Leila, you take care and tell that husband of yours that he is a lucky man."

"I sure will," Leila said and Rayshon walked out of the door.

"*Yeah, I'll tell him whenever I get a chance to have a conversation with him again,*" Leila said out loud once Ray was on the other side of the door. She had only been married for six years and as soon as she got pregnant Devon made an exit, not because of the baby and responsibilities, but because he was no longer interested in her.

It started out subtle at first, but it didn't take Devon long before he got his own place. First it was staying out super late and then turned into not coming home at all. By her third month, she was on her own. The day Deja was born, Devon swore he would get his act together and come home, but that was three months ago. Three months of lying, false hope and fake promises.

The major problem with Devon was the in and out. One minute he was in and wanted to make it work and the next minute he was out. Finally, after all of the drama, he told Leila that he was going to file for divorce, but she still has yet to see that happen.

Leila didn't even flinch, when he said the word *"divorce,"* because it had almost been two years since she even considered them husband and wife. She already cried all she could cry, prayed all she could pray and pleaded all she could plead for him to come back to her and for them to be a family again.

She still loved and wanted her husband - yes, but she finally had come to terms that they were over. She stopped wishing and hoping and started setting the alarm on her security system at night with her new code. She wasn't hurting financially at all because Devon did still support her and Deja and even if he didn't; her mother left her a nice piece of change when she passed three years ago.

Leila was working at a publishing company in the editing department before she purchased the store. She always had a love for reading and after her mom died, she took some of her money and opened herself a little bookstore. It wasn't as busy as a Barnes & Noble's, but she did well.

In addition, Devon wasn't what we called poor either. He was senior partner at a cellular company and he was pretty much set. At times, she wished he was broke, so he could at least need her for her money, but that was not the case and even after having his first and only child didn't make him want to be with her.

They met in college and dated forever. After they married, things were good for the most part, but after a little weight here and a few pounds there, he changed. He didn't want to take Leila with him anywhere anymore and the more depressed her marriage made her the more weight she put on.

When she got pregnant, that really turned him off. He made comments to her in the beginning like, *"Man, now you're really going to blow up,"* or when he asked the doctor, *"So doc, how much weight does a baby actually put on a woman, generally?"* Leila wanted to slap him. She knew she was not the size ten he married, but she thought she was still pretty.

"What's your problem?" she asked him when they got in the car after leaving the doctor's office.

"My problem is you not wanting to go to the gym or how you act like you don't realize you're not looking the way you did on our wedding day. That is my problem. You are tipping the scale Lei and you act like you don't see how big you have gotten. I mean you are getting bigger and bigger," he said coldly, being his usual insulting self.

"Devon I am pregnant," she said in her own defense.

"Yes, but you are only six or seven weeks Lei. That forty or fifty pounds you have gained since we got married has nothing to do with this pregnancy. Only God knows how many pounds you're going to pack on during this pregnancy," he said, not sparing her feelings.

"Devon I know I'm not a size ten anymore, don't you think I know that? I'm not some fat ugly beast and I am tired of you acting like you are so disgusted or ashamed of me. You don't have a problem with my weight when you wanna get some. My weight doesn't seem to bother you then. When you wanna please your dick, my weight doesn't seem to stop you from jumping in me."

"Oh so I'm not supposed to want to touch you either?"

"That's not what I mean Devon. If you love me enough to still wanna make love to me, you should love me enough to still wanna take me out with you or wanna spend more time with me and not always put me down. You never hold me anymore. You don't take me places like you used to and I am so tired of you making impudent remarks about me. If you loved me, you wouldn't do that," she said, crying.

"Well maybe I don't," he said callously.

"What? Maybe you don't what Devon?" she asked, hoping he didn't mean what she thought he was saying.

"Love you," he said and Leila's heart dropped.

"What?" she asked softly and he didn't say another word. After that, things got worse. He slowly moved out and Leila cried herself to sleep every night. She woke up every morning wishing she had never married Devon. He was the only man that she ever loved and his love was conditional. When he visits his daughter, he looks at Leila with this look of disappointment and disgust and she hates to be in the same room with him.

She makes a point to have something to run out to do or she does something in another room to avoid him all together. Therefore, when he told her about his plans to file for a divorce she told him, *"So be it."*

II

Leila was standing on the porch waiting for Devon to bring Deja to her. On Saturday's he had her, so Leila could work at her store since he worked Monday through Friday. During the work-week, Deja went to Emoni's daycare center, a few blocks down from the bookstore. That made it so convenient for Leila and she was comfortable with taking her there.

When she got home, she had a few things to do, so she was hoping he'd come a little later so she could get some things done around the house, but Devon acted like he had such a busy social life and had to bring the baby right away. She hadn't been in the house for two minutes before he was blowing his horn in the driveway.

He walked up the steps and handed Deja to Leila in her car seat without a *"hello"* or *"good evening."* He was too busy with the conversation that he was having on his Bluetooth to say hello. Leila figured the call was too important for him to pause to simply say hi.

"Good evening Devon," Leila said speaking to him first. If she hadn't said anything she knew he may have walked away without saying a word to her.

"Yeah, yeah, hey - hold on a sec," he said to the person he was on the phone with. "She just ate about forty-five minutes ago.

She was grunting in the car on the way, so she may need a new diaper," he said and walked away. Still not acknowledging Leila's *'good evening.'*

"And how are you Devon?" Leila asked attempting to get a little conversation out of him.

"I'm fine," he said and kept walking. He proceeded to talk to his Bluetooth as he got back into his Jaguar and pulled out of the driveway. Leila was still standing on the porch with the baby and diaper bag. She watched his taillights down the street and she finally went inside.

She sat the baby in her carrier on the table and put the diaper bag in the chair, *"Hey, sweetie pie, how ya doing girl?"* she asked and Deja was smiling beautifully. *"Aw, I see how you are doing stinky girl,"* she said, walking her up to her nursery. She strapped her down on her changing table, went into the hall bathroom and started the water. She put the baby tub into the big tub and filled it with warm water.

She went back into the nursery to undress her little doll. *"There we go baby. Let's get this stinky stuff off my baby,"* she said and Deja was full of laughs, kicking her little legs. She gave her a bath and shampooed her hair. After she lotion her up, she sat in her rocker to nurse her. *"I guess it's you and me kid, again on a lonely Saturday night,"* she said sadly. After she burped, she put her down in her crib.

Deja was a good baby, so she was content while Leila did a few things around the house. She went back to check on her and she was sleeping. Leila checked her diaper and hated to change her while she was sleeping, but she had to. She made it through the diaper change without disturbing her too bad because she fell right back to sleep. It was only eight o'clock and Leila was bored. She went downstairs and looked over all the DVDs to find something to watch, but out of eight hundred movies, none of them she felt like watching.

She went back to her room and climbed into bed. She flipped through the channels and landed on the Cosby show, *'how can Claire and Cliff be so happy? Maybe because Claire never got fat,'* she said to herself and muted the volume. She grabbed her book and picked up where she left off.

Once she got deep into it, her phone rang and it was Devon. She looked at the clock and it was after nine. *'What in the hell did he want?'* she wondered before she answered.

"Hello," she said wryly.

"Hey Lei this is Devon."

"I know. What is it?"

"Well I got DJ's binky and I'm going to bring it back for you," he said and Leila was looking like *'you got to be kidding me.'*

"Devon, Deja has three or four binky's around here. Besides, she is already asleep."

"Are you sure, because I'm about five minutes away?"

"I'm sure. We are good."

"Well let me come by anyway so I can see her."

"Devon what are you - on drugs? She is sleep; did you not hear me say that?"

"Okay I'll be there in five," he said and hung up before Leila could dispute. She got up and put on a pair of sweats. She had on a tank top but didn't bother to change it because it was only Devon. Her hair was pulled back and she had on her glasses and she didn't attempt to fix herself up for Devon. He rang the bell as she was walking down the stairs. She opened the door and he was standing there with the binky in his hand.

"Thanks," she said, taking it from him and walking away. He followed her inside and closed the door.

"Where's DJ?" he asked, like he was retarded.

"Where do you think Devon? She is in her crib," Leila said, giving him much attitude, walking into the kitchen - and he was right behind her. She poured herself a glass of juice not offering him anything.

"Well Lei, she could have been in her bassinet or in our bed. I don't know," he said.

"Well she is not in my bed Devon, she is in her crib," she said, looking at him like he was crazy. What was with the *'our bed'* madness, she thought to herself. He hadn't lived there in months.

"Well I'm going to go up and see her."

"Go ahead," Leila said and didn't bother to follow him up. She sat on the sofa in the family room and turned on the television. She never had any problems with Devon seeing Deja and she never denied him the opportunity to come over if he wanted to spend time with her, but why was he trying to see her when he knew she was sleeping?

After a little while, she wondered what was taking him so long to come back down. She put the remote down and went up to see what he was doing. Maybe he woke her and was just holding her. When she reached the top of the steps, she went into the nursery and no Devon. She tapped on the hall bathroom and no one answered.

She went back to look in on Deja and she was still in her crib sleeping peacefully. She walked slowly down the hall to her master bedroom and she knew she was going to have to cuss his ass out.

"No, no, no, get the hell up outta my bed, Negro!" she yelled. Devon thought he was slick and Leila wasn't having it. She vowed he'd never touch her again unless they were going to get back together and here he was pulling another move on her, like she had *'stupid,'* written across her forehead.

"Come on Lei, I need you tonight," he said pitifully.

"Devon please, you can't be serious?" she asked him, trying to keep a straight face.

"Why wouldn't I be? Lei I love you and you know that. Things are just difficult right now between us, but I never fell out of love with you. I was just so attracted to the woman I married and you changed Lei. You changed," he said sadly.

"Devon my exterior changed - yes, but I am the same woman you married. I've gained weight – yes, but that was not an excuse for you to walk out on me and I am sick and tired of you treating me like your doormat. You can't come over here whenever you feel like you wanna screw me and expect me to get all excited for you."

"That's not it Lei. Do you think I don't miss you? Do you think I don't love you? I've never stop loving you Lei."

"Then why aren't you here?" she yelled and he didn't respond. He sat there looking crazy and didn't say a word. "Exactly," she said and walked over to her side of the bed, sat down and he moved over closer to her.

"Lei please, I didn't mean to upset you. I just want you to understand I'm still in love with you, but I wish I had the old you."

"Well you can't have any of the new me tonight," she said sternly and got up.

"Can I at least stay tonight please? I am tired Lei and I don't want to drive all the way across town. Honestly, I don't want to be by myself tonight. I will get up with the baby and give you a break. Just let me stay."

"Fine, you can stay and Devon don't touch me okay, I'm not in the mood to be with you like that and you betta get up with Deja too. I'm not playing with you," she said and went downstairs to turn everything off and set the alarm. She went to shower and climbed into bed. She drifted off to sleep and of course as the night progressed their bodies made contact and the feeling of his hardness pressed against her ass made it hard to resist his moves.

Before she could fight it or dispute his advances, he was deep inside of her love doing what she didn't want him to do. She moaned and panted because it felt so good to have him inside of her and she wished it was not a temporary situation. By the time he was done working her body over she was exhausted.

He did what he said he would do by taking care of the baby when she got up for her feeding, so that allowed Leila to get good sleep. The next morning he fixed breakfast and hung around for a while and they played husband and wife for a few hours. It was so temporary and as usual he made his normal exit around two that afternoon.

Leila shut the door behind him and hated herself for allowing him to have his way with her. She wanted to be over him and completely done, but he was her only source of dick. Most times she'd shut Devon down with the quickness, but last night wasn't one of those times. She let her body get its own way.

She went upstairs to get Deja and went into her bedroom. She realized Devon had conveniently forgotten his watch on the nightstand of what used to be his side of the bed. For some reason she didn't know why he still had a lot of his stuff there, even though he had a condo on the other side of town. Many times Leila would promise she'd gather his stuff and box it all up, but time had gone by and she still had not. She took the watch and placed it into his top nightstand drawer where she normally put all of his personal items that he left behind after their rendezvous. He'd always say, *"I'll get it next time,"* but somehow next time had not come around for him to get any of his items.

The day rolled by and by nightfall Leila was sad that Devon had gotten her goods and totally ignored her the rest of the day. She fought the urge to call him after she put Deja down for the night. *"It's okay DJ, we are gonna be fine without him,"* she said, walking out of her baby's nursery. Her sweet innocent infant had no clue of how messed up things were. She was too small to see that her parents were not together and had so many issues. If she only knew how much pain her momma was in, she'd probably hate her daddy and that thought made Leila relieved that she was a baby.

When Leila got into bed, she closed her eyes and thanked God for giving her such a good baby. People told her if you cry a lot during your pregnancy, your baby will be a crybaby and Leila knew for a fact that that myth was a lie because she cried her entire pregnancy and Deja was not a crybaby. She was a good baby and Leila knew she was fortunate.

She made sure the baby monitor was on before she got ready to go to sleep and then she decided to try Devon before she called it a night. Of course she got his voicemail and she didn't bother to leave him a message. She didn't get angry at all, because she was accustomed to his behavior. She fell asleep easily and her two a.m. baby alarm was right on schedule.

Deja was up for her feeding and even if the monitor didn't work, Leila could hear her crying from a mile away. She dragged herself out of bed and went in to take care of her baby. It was hard, but in the end, it was all worth it.

III

"Ten, nine, eight, seven, six, five, come on, three, two and one, good job," Rayshon said to his client. He really hated this session, but it was the best paying session he had. Christa was a gorgeous vanilla complexioned woman with a dot here and there on her skin that people referred to as beauty marks, but Ray only saw them as moles. She had been his client for four years and had referred tons of her model friends to him.

She was 5'9" and didn't have more than 1 percent of body fat on her toned body. She had long wavy hair that she sometimes had blown out straight. She was of mixed race, Korean and Black and she was always teased, called a war baby because her daddy was in the military and married a Korean woman. Although no wars were going on when she was conceived, she was always teased with the same joke.

Ray liked her and admired her beauty, but he didn't like her romantically. Although she was gorgeous, she had much attitude; nothing humble about her. She was a bitch to the tenth power and she wanted Ray badly, so he couldn't stand to be around her most of the time. She would always flirt with him and make comments about how she could get any man she wanted.

She even went as far as saying he was gay. She told one of the girls she referred that he had to be a dookie chaser if he didn't want her, which is one hundred percent wrong. Ray loved women and he was as masculine as they come inside and out. From his head to his toes, he was the tenth degree of manly.

He just has a rule; never date any of his clients. Dating a client or a co-worker to him was the worst thing for anyone's business. Just like word of mouth, it can either build your business or annihilate your business. Client by client; through referrals of top-notch service or client you made a big mistake hooking up with ruins your business name because things didn't go their way.

Luckily for him, he provided his clients with that top-notch service and he didn't have to work as an employee at the gym where he had started anymore. He could now come and go as he pleased according to his schedule and his appointments. He was set up at home and things were marvelous, so he had no intention on dating any of his clients and Christa was one of those types of clients who would bring a brother's business down.

She was what she thought of herself as popular because she was a local model and did a lot of work in the Chicago area, so she had a li'l clout and she believed the hype and preferred to workout at Ray's loft, where he converted his upstairs to a training area. He had a treadmill, elliptical, bike, free weights, a bench, jump ropes, mats and bands. It was a private and profitable set up, but he hated having her and a couple other clients there alone because it never failed that they thought they could seduce him.

Christa met with Ray at least four times a week and didn't have a set schedule due to her so called career, so she made her appointments weekly according to her schedule and his availability. She paid more for the flex schedule that he worked with her on and they were both happy with their arrangement. The only thing that made Ray unhappy was the constant flirting. She'd try him every session and he'd turn her down every time. If it had not been for the good money and heavy referrals and the fact that they had a contract, he would have let her go a long time ago. Since his goal was to open his own fitness center one day, he put up with a lot of shit that he didn't want to tolerate.

"So, I'll see you Wednesday?" Ray asked, walking Christa to the door. Her session had run a couple minutes over and he only had three minutes to prepare for his next client.

"Yes Wednesday or if you'd like to see me sooner," she asked seductively moving closer to him. She was on a mission to break him down because he was the first and only man that she'd ever met that didn't try to sleep with her. There was no way she wasn't going to make him want her, because she definitely wanted him.

"Christa we do this every session. I told you I don't date my clients," he said, backing up.

"Well I don't wanna be your client anymore," she threatened again for the one hundredth time.

"Yes you do," he said, smiling.

"No I don't. You are fired. Now let's go and get this over with," she said, moving in for the kill and he stopped her dead in her tracks.

"Well Ms. Thang you can't fire me because we have a contract and you know I'm the best," he said, boasting.

"Damn Ray, why are you so stubborn? I know you want this," she said, rubbing herself.

"Bye Christa, I gotta get ready for my next session."

"Alright Mr. Do the Right Thing. You gon' give in to me sooner or later because I know you wanna taste this," she said smiling and going for the door.

"Well until then, I'll see you on Wednesday," he said and closed the door behind her. She was fine and he could tap that ass right, but he didn't want to go there with her because he didn't want a woman like Christa. She'd be more than a handful and he didn't want a relationship or to be involved with a woman that he knew one day he may want to shake the shit out of.

He wiped down the area with the sanitizing wipes and dashed to the door to open it for Loran. She was one of the chicks that Christa referred to him and she was just as bad, but he knew how to handle their asses. He let her in and they got started right away. She had a nice body and was a dime, but she always had a weave.

Ray didn't understand why sista's always had to have a weave. He really hated his clients with the weaves that always complained about sweating their weave out. That drove him insane. He'd heard that so many times from his clients. How did they expect to lose weight and get in shape without sweating? That was one of his things, can't date a woman with weave.

After Loran's session, he had two more clients to see before he had some free time. Once he was done with his morning sessions, he showered and decided he'd run back to the bookstore to get the other book that he should have gotten before, but didn't and didn't remember why he didn't.

He pulled his Tahoe into a parking space and noticed a sign on the door that said, *"Be back in fifteen minutes."* He sat in his truck and waited for a few moments and then a gray Armada pulled into the private parking space on the side of the building. When she got out, he noticed it was Leila. She looked kind of different he thought. She didn't have on her glasses and she had on some makeup and her hair was down. She was actually pretty, he thought to himself while he checked her out.

She took the sign down and he watched her walk to the back through the huge glass window and imagined how he could sculpt her thick body to perfection if given the chance. Give her definition in her arms, while leaving her perfect breasts the way they were, she'd be a showstopper he thought to himself and got out of his SUV. He walked into the store and the bell on the door alerted her that someone had come in.

"I'll be with you in a moment," she yelled from the back. He walked over to the counter and saw his card on top of the stack of business cards. At least she didn't throw it away, he was thinking to himself when she came out of the back office.

"I'm sorry to have kept you waiting," she said, not realizing it was him.

"Hey Leila," he said and smiled.

"Hi, how are you?" she asked and didn't return the warm smile that he had given her.

"Oh, I'm good. I just wanted to come by and pick up that other book you recommended."

"Okay, I can get that for you," she said and came from behind the counter. He followed her and watched her every move.

"Here you are," she said, handing it to him. "This is the right one, isn't it?"

"Yes this is it."

"Is there anything else you'd like for me to get for you?"

"Yes there is actually," he said and she wished she never said that.

"And that is?" she asked impatiently.

"Well first I know you said that you were not interested in hiring a personal trainer, but what if I gave you a session for free? I mean, you can't beat free. And if you don't have a good time and not feel motivated to come again, I'll leave you alone."

"No...," she said, walking away. "Not interested."

"No? What do you mean *'No?'* It's a free session and trust me my love, my sessions are not cheap."

"No thank you," she said that time with even more attitude.

"Leila come on now, what is the big deal? It's a free session. It'll be fun. I mean, what do you have to lose?"

"What is your problem?" she asked, losing patience.

"Hold on Leila. I don't have a problem I was just trying to offer you something that might change your life."

"What is with you guys? Am I just that disgusting to look at that I must get to the gym right now? What if I like how I look? Why are people so worried about a woman's size? We are not all skinny okay? We can't look like Beyonce," she yelled and Ray was stumped.

"Listen Leila, I'm sorry okay? I wasn't trying to offend you or imply that you need to lose weight. I see women all day in various shapes and sizes and trust me; I know y'all can't all look like Beyonce. I understand that women have problem areas in some cases, no matter how hard you work at it; it will never achieve that look you would like for it to achieve. I understand and know that some things are not physically possible to achieve with diet and exercise. You are a very attractive woman and I'd be a fool if I saw you out and not notice you.

"So, I'm sorry if I offended you. I'm just in the business to help people - not just women - get healthy and get into shape. All of my clients are not skinny and trust I haven't came across any Beyonce, not naturally anyway," he said jokingly and smiled. "They've been nipped and tucked here and there, trust me," he said and the tension in her face loosened.

"You are fine just the way you are and I'm not here to make you skinny. I just wanna motivate you to have a healthier heart. If you work with me only thirty minutes with cardio alone, that will change your life I'm telling you and your husband too," he said, trying to make her feel comfortable.

"Look, I understand what you are trying to say trust me. I'm just a little sore right now, so I didn't mean to snap off on you like that," she said, giving him a little smile.

"No, don't sweat it. I'm cool; I just want you to try one session. Not commit yourself, but just one. I know you'd love it."

"Okay Rayshon maybe one. I just can't guarantee you anything. I may give it a try."

"Well you have my card and as I said before, your husband too. It is a lot of fun for couples to do it together and my married clients have a blast."

"Well I may, but I can't say my husband will," she said, knowing damn well that Devon wouldn't be coming with her. They weren't doing anything together because they weren't together.

"Okay that's cool, just give me a call so we can set something up."

"I will," she said and proceeded to ring him up for the book. "Maybe if I have fun, I'll sign up."

"Well I'll have your contract ready; because I know you are gonna wanna come back."

"Hold on Rayshon. You are getting ahead of yourself."

"Oh my bad," he said taking the bag.

"Thanks for stopping in and keep us in mind for your next book purchase," she said.

"I most definitely will and I hope to hear from you soon," he said and he left.

IV

"Come on Devon," Leila said, looking at her watch. It was five 'til eight and Devon was twenty-five minutes late. She had plans to go to the movies with her girlfriend Renee and Devon was supposed to get the baby for her. Since the next day was Saturday and she had to open the store, he agreed to keep the baby all night.

He finally pulled up into the driveway and it was a woman in the passenger seat and Leila almost passed out. He never went that far to bring someone to her house with him before and she was pissed at the idea of him actually doing it. When he got out the car, he could see the fire in Leila's eyes as he walked up the walkway to the porch.

Leila could see the young woman clearly, because the bright censor light that was attached to her garage was shining into Devon's car. She was pretty and she was definitely slim. Very petite and that made Leila even more mad.

"Who in the hell is that Devon?" she asked him with her teeth clinched, not trying to bring attention to herself. She wanted to slap the piss out of him for bringing some female with him to her house to pick up their daughter.

"Don't even trip Lei, she's a co-worker. Our meeting ran over and since I was running late I had to swing by here to get Deja before

I took her back to her car," he said, trying to take the baby's carrier out of Leila's hand, but she held on tight.

"Don't lie to me Devon. I'm not stupid."

"Lei please give me the baby and calm down. You can come and meet her if you like."

"I don't wanna meet that trick. Do you know how many mistresses smile in women faces and fuck their husbands behind their backs?" Leila asked in a louder tone. She didn't want to show out, but she wanted the mistress to know she wasn't new to the game.

"Lei you are insane, you know that? I will talk to you later."

"Later when Devon?" she asked him, still not releasing the grip she had on the baby's carrier.

"Lei come on now, don't make a scene. Come to the car; you can meet her. She works in our accounting department. I wouldn't disrespect you like that Lei. You know I'm not that foolish," he said lying, but she believed him. He was crazy, but not that crazy - was what she thought. She let the carrier go, straightened up her face and walked out to the car.

"Hi I'm Leila, Devon's wife."

"Hello Leila, I'm Michelle. I've heard a lot about you," she said and Leila wondered how she had heard a lot about her when she and Devon were just co-workers.

"Oh have you?" Leila asked, giving Devon a look out the corner of her eyes.

"Yes, on the ride over here Devon was telling me what a wonderful mother you are and about your bookstore," she said, cleaning it up, Leila thought to herself.

"Oh did he?"

"Yeah and I'd love to check out your store. I mean, I love to read," she said with a smile.

"Well whenever you wanna stop in. We are open every day

except Sundays."

"I will," Michelle said and Leila saw that Devon was done strapping the baby in.

"Well it was nice to meet you Michelle."

"You too…," she said with a bright smile. Leila knew it was fake and she knew she was sucking Devon's dick.

"Alright Devon, I'll call you tonight to check on DJ."

"Okay and you enjoy your movie and tell Renee I said hello," he said and put on his seat belt.

"Okay, drive safely and you have a good night Michelle."

"You too Lei," she said and Leila looked at her strange and Devon cranked the engine. Who was this bitch to call her *'Lei'* like she knew her? Leila backed away from the car to keep from saying another word. She watched them drive off with her baby girl and wondered how long this little five pound; twelve-ounce bitch had been fucking her husband.

She didn't spend much time on wondering about Michelle and Devon because it didn't matter; there was nothing she could do to stop Devon from doing what he wanted, so she tried to not think of them. She went inside and called Renee and told her they would have to catch a later movie and Renee decided it would be better to go a different night because she wasn't trying to go that late. She hung up with Renee with an attitude because she was disappointed that they couldn't hang out for a while; Leila definitely didn't want to be in the house that night.

She went into the bathroom, undressed, looked at herself in the mirror and her reflection made her sad. She was out of shape and fat, she thought to herself. She thought about Michelle, the bomb-shell that was in her husband's passenger seat rolling around with him and she started to cry. "That's why you left me?" she yelled at the mirror and she sobbed.

She put on her robe, went downstairs and poured herself a

glass of wine. She was pumped for a few days, so she could enjoy a couple glasses. She turned on the radio and found herself sitting and crying. After her little pity party, she turned off everything, climbed the steps and went into her bedroom. She climbed into her empty king-sized bed and pulled up the covers.

She picked up the phone, called Devon and he finally answered on the fifth ring.

"Hey Lei, what's up?"

"Nothing how is my baby?"

"She is good. I just put her down about ten minutes ago," he said and Leila heard a voice in the background.

"Devon who is that?" she demanded.

"Nobody," he said.

"Come on Devon, nobody? Is that Michelle?" she yelled.

"No Lei I told you...," he tried to say.

"Devon don't lie to me. Tell me the truth. Are you with Michelle?" she demanded.

"Can we talk about this tomorrow?"

"Hell no, we are still married Devon."

"Lei please, I have people here," he said, trying to talk low.

"Oh so you are entertaining? Why didn't you invite me over? Why wasn't I invited to your little party?" she yelled. She was a little tipsy from the three glasses of wine she drank and she was upset that he was living the life and she was already in bed by ten on a Friday night. "How are you taking care of Deja and having a party Devon?"

"Listen Lei, I gotta go. My daughter is fine. I am responsible enough to have guest and take care of my child and it is not a party."

"Devon, why are you doing this to me? I love you so, so much and you act like you don't even care," she said crying.

"Look Leila, tomorrow. I'll call you tomorrow," he said and

then he hung up.

"Devon, Devon…," she said and she put the phone down. She didn't bother calling him back because she knew it wouldn't do any good. She got on her knees and cried 'til her head ached. She begged God for strength. She just didn't want to hurt anymore. She didn't want to love him anymore. She wanted to be okay with who she was and how she looked. She wanted peace.

She got up, got back into bed and she cried herself to sleep again. That was how it was for her the past couple of years and she prayed that it would soon change and the crying herself to sleep would one day come to an end.

V

The next day Leila went to work and avoided calling Devon at all costs. She was embarrassed of how she acted on the phone with him for one and for two she didn't want to hear his voice. If he wanted a divorce, she would give him the divorce. She no longer cared about him or who he was with. She just wanted to focus on herself.

That morning she had taken off her beautiful ring and put it into her jewelry box. It was no point in faking the funk and walking around claiming to be married to a man that left her. She mostly wore it to keep from looking like a single mom when she was by herself with the baby and now she didn't care what people thought because she was what she was: a single mom.

She felt free for a change and she didn't want to keep walking around being unnoticed and ignored by folks. She set up a hair appointment and decided to get her nails and feet done too. It was the third week of August, winter was around the corner and she didn't have any winter clothes that fit so she knew the stores would be on her list. She left Renee at the bookstore and told her she'd be back before closing.

Since she was a sixteen, she had no idea how hard it was to find clothes in her size. Every rack she went to made her upset. She remembered when she was small and how she could just grab what she wanted off the rack and go home without even trying them on, but those days were gone and she was wondering how did plus size women make it with cute clothes being so limited?

She felt like an outcast and she hated she had to try on everything. She managed to leave the mall with several things, but it was work. She didn't care because all she wanted was a start on her new attitude and new look. After she got her hair, nails and feet done, she felt better. She went back to the store and Renee was impressed.

"Wow girl, you look good. I almost didn't recognize you."

"You think so?"

"Yes ma'am. I should have gone with you instead of hanging around here all day. I mean the hair, the makeup and the new threads - you look like a model."

"Gon' now girl," she said.

"For real, I should have gone too."

"Were we busy today?"

"Yes and no, we had spurts. Oh and a fine brother came in here asking about you Ms. Leila. Told me to tell you that he's still waiting for you to set up that appointment," Renee said and Leila knew exactly who she was talking about.

"Yeah," Leila said and she thought about taking him on. She could at least try it.

"Oh yes and my Lord he was fine," Renee said.

"He's alright."

"So you know who I'm talking about?"

"Yes, his card is right there. He's a personal trainer."

"He can be my personal everything. Shit girl, he's like damn! I couldn't stop staring. If my husband hadda been here, he would have snatched my eyeballs out," she said and they laughed.

"He's okay. Devon is finer than he is," Leila said, going back to Devon. He was in her heart.

"Yeah let you tell it. You stuck on Devon's behind. If you didn't know Devon and saw them both walking down the street, who would you pick?"

"Devon…," she said.

"Chile please, Devon gotcha hooked."

"No he doesn't. I don't even like Devon like that anymore Renee. You know we are done."

"Yeah I know he is, but are you?"

"Well we were married."

"Keyword: were," Renee said.

"Whatever Renee, you just don't like Devon."

"No, I do like Devon. That is Deja's father. I just don't like the way he treats Deja's mother."

"Well that is in the past and now I'm moving on with my life."

"And you can start by making that appointment."

"That has nothing to do with me moving on Renee."

"I know, but after looking at him for what, an hour a day, you'll be like *'Devon who?'* she said and they laughed.

"You are a mess," Leila said and went to lock the door. She turned out the *'Open'* sign and she and Renee closed the bookstore. She and Renee were going to go and see that movie that they had missed the night before. Before Leila left the store, she grabbed the card that Rayshon had left and stuck it into her purse.

When Leila got home, she called Devon to let him know it

was okay to bring Deja home, but she got his voicemail. She left him a message letting him know she was home, then she tried on the outfits again that she had purchased earlier. She still had on her makeup and her hair looked good. It was nice and bouncy and her new highlights complimented her pretty face. She got her brows arched and her eyes were bright and open and she was happy for a change.

She stood in the mirror, admiring herself after she put on a new outfit and she smiled because she felt like she looked good. She knew she wasn't the same size she used to be, but she was wearing it well. Her vanilla complexion and slightly slanted eyes drew attention to her face. She had smooth skin with only a couple of blemishes from the occasional menstrual breakout that didn't require a lot of foundation to cover up.

She had a slim nose with high cheekbones and her full lips were beautiful with the dark red lipstick that she had on. Her natural brown hair was always long past her shoulders and she was glad she made the risky decision to layer it and changed the old boring color. She was checking herself out in a pair of tight jeans and creamy color sweater when her doorbell rang. She ran down and looked through the peephole and it was Devon. Damn, he must have been on his way to her house, she thought as she opened the door and Devon's jaw dropped to the floor. When he saw Leila and how good she was looking, he just stood at the door.

"Come on in," she said and walked away. He walked in behind her and her body looked reshaped in her jeans. He was used to seeing her in maternity clothes or in sweats with her hair pulled back with no makeup and in her glasses. Now she was looking sexy and voluptuous and he liked what he saw. She didn't have on her glasses and Devon was turned on. He put the baby on the table in her carrier and put her bag on the floor.

Leila carried on as if he wasn't there. She didn't have anything to say to him. She came into the family room to get her baby, but she was sleep. She took her out of her carrier and started talking to her, trying to wake her, but apparently Deja was too tired, so she put her in her bassinet that was downstairs instead of taking her to her nursery.

"Damn Lei where you been?"

"To the movies," she said, not stopping to chat.

"With whom?" he asked.

"Excuse me?"

"With who…? You were not with Renee looking like that."

"Why can't I be out with Renee because I made an effort today to look human?"

"No, because you look like you trying to entice a man."

"Well I am grown and on my own."

"What the hell does that mean?" he yelled.

"It means I am going to start living for me and start worrying about my future, not our future. Your life is going on without me and I should be going on without you."

"Wait a minute. We are still married."

"Yeah, that's what I said to you last night right before you hung up in my face. So now I'm living my life for me Devon…, me," she said, pointing at herself.

"Come on Lei, I never said that there was no chance for us to get back together."

"Yeah, your lips didn't, but your actions do."

"So now you out dating, is that it? Some dude done whispered some mack daddy bullshit in your ear and now were done?"

"No Devon, you got it all wrong. You see, I decided to stop waiting on you to control what I do and whom I do it with. If you cared so much, we'd be together under one roof living as husband and wife instead of you dropping DJ off. You'd be here for us and here to make me feel like a woman. You told me *fuck you* the day you forwarded your mail. So, I will say this so you can understand," she said, walking closer to him. "The ball is not in your possession anymore and you are not going to score another point with making Leila feel bad, nor will you hurt me again. I am done crying myself to sleep every night. I am done with wishing and praying and hoping. Devon I am done with you," she said and walked into the kitchen.

"Oh so you want a divorce?" he asked, following her into the kitchen.

"No Devon, I want you. I want my marriage, but I am sick and tired of these games, so if you are not here to tell me we are going to be together and be a family and make our marriage work, this conversation is over."

"Just like that Lei? You have nothing else to say to me?"

"What do you want me to do Devon? I mean seriously, tell me what do you suppose I do? You are the one that say you wanna divorce and then you don't file and then you come back around here giving me hope that we are going to work it out. What do I do Devon huh? I mean really, just keep spending my nights alone wondering when or if Devon is coming home? Do you expect me to really let you keep coming by and getting some ass when you want it and then taking off? Come on Devon, tell me?"

"No, I expect you to act like a mother and give your man a minute to get himself together. Do you think you need to be bringing strange men around my daughter?"

"That's all you are worried about Devon? Another man in my face, why worry about that Devon? I'm a smart woman and a good mother and I wouldn't expose my daughter to anything that is not appropriate. Deja is three months Devon, so please don't go there with that nonsense. You don't have problem with having my baby around Michelle."

"Michelle is a co-worker," he said lying to her face. Michelle was the reason he finally got his condo because she told him if he didn't move out and leave Leila like he promised she was going to cut him off. Now she was putting pressure on him to get his divorce and that he didn't like because he still wasn't sure if he wanted a divorce, nor did he know if he really wanted to be with her.

"Yeah whatever Devon," she said and walked away and he followed behind her. She went upstairs to remove her clothes. She took off her pants and he noticed she was wearing a thong - and he was out done. Who gave her this confidence, were the thoughts going through his mind.

"Oh I see you've been shopping?"

"Yep and I see you're still here."

"Now you're putting me out?"

"You're being ridiculous Devon," she said, trying to walk by him, but he blocked her path. "Now move," she said, pushing by him.

"We are not over Lei."

"Then prove it," she said with a challenge.

"What…?"

"If we are not over go and get your stuff and come home tonight."

"It's not that simple Lei."

"It is that simple Devon. Get in your car - no better yet take off your clothes, get in the bed and get comfortable and in the morning we get up, have breakfast and then go get your things and then we take it one day at a time and we make our marriage work," she said, standing right in his face. She looked so beautiful and had sincere love in her eyes for him, but he couldn't lie to her. He had things going on at that point that he needed to resolve before he could pour himself back one hundred percent into their marriage. As much as he loved her, he could not come back that night.

"I want to Lei, but…," he tried to say, but she didn't let him finish.

"Then we are over. Please show yourself out."

"Lei baby please….," he tried to say, but she went into the

bathroom and shut the door. She didn't shed one tear and she was determined not to let him see her cry. He was at a loss when she came out the bathroom and walked around totally ignoring his efforts to talk to her. He finally realized that she was serious and he grabbed his keys and headed for the door.

"I love you Lei," he said and she didn't feel a thing. His words were just words with no meaning behind them. He stood there in the doorway a few moments and she got her baby and went up the stairs. She didn't go back down to lock the door 'til she heard his car pull out of the driveway.

VI

After cleaning her house and doing a few loads of laundry, Leila decided that she and Deja would get dress and go out for a while. She had no particular place she wanted to go, but she knew she didn't want to be in the house. She dressed her baby first and went into her room and made herself look glamorous for their outing. She was so used to being in the house on Sundays the entire day, so she was excited to be up and dressed and out of the house.

She got in the truck and decided she'd go to the park and then by the mall. She was smiling when she put on her shades, because she felt like a sexy mom that day. Her hair was fresh and she managed to do her makeup well and she admired her reflection in the rearview mirror. She cranked the engine; she turned to look over her shoulder to pull out and remembered that her baby's stroller was with Devon.

She wanted to avoid him at all costs, but God wasn't making it easy on her because in order to walk in the park or through the mall she had to have her stroller. She got on the main road and headed toward Devon's condo. She didn't bother calling because she didn't want to even hear his voice. When she got there, there was a little two-seat BMW in his guest-parking stall, so she parked in the stall across because she knew she'd only be a minute.

She got on his floor, walked down the hall and rang the bell of his unit. When the door opened, she wished she had called because it was Michelle and she didn't look like she was dressed for work, but Leila kept her cool. She didn't go off because she knew she was with Devon from the moment she met her.

"Umm hi, umm, Leila. Umm how ya' doing?" Michelle said nervously.

"I am fine and you?"

"I'm good; I was on my way out. I just stopped by to pick up some papers."

"Okay, where is Devon? I need my baby's stroller," Leila said, not even trying to go in. She had her baby in her arms and she knew getting crazy would only frighten her baby.

"Hold on...," she said and went closer to the hall and called out his name. He came out in a pair of shorts and no shirt. He was in total shock to see Leila and the baby at the door.

"Lei..., hey..., come in...," he said, trying to play it cool. He rushed over to the door and the look on Leila's face was not pleasant. "Hey Deja, how is daddy's baby girl?" he asked grabbing Deja's little hand and she started to smile at her daddy. "Come in Lei, why are you standing in the door?"

"I just need to get DJ's stroller," Leila said, doing an awesome job not crying. She wasn't hurt; she was more tired and emotionally drained to even react to the situation.

"Sure, let me...," he said, scrambling for his keys.

"You may wanna grab a shirt lover man and Michelle it was good seeing you again," Leila said and turned to walk away without allowing Michelle to say bye to her. She overheard Devon asking Michelle why did she open the door and Michelle say she didn't know it was Leila. She explained that she thought it was the delivery guy with their food, Leila heard while she stood waiting for the elevator. Devon was down in a matter of minutes to get the stroller, trying to explain.

"Save it Devon, I don't care to hear it. Just get the stroller man," Leila told him while she put her baby in her car seat.

"Trust me, there is nothing going on up there. I promise it's not what you think," he said lying while he put the stroller in the back of Leila's Armada.

"Well Devon, I don't care. I am drained. You've sucked every ounce of energy out of me. Just go back upstairs to your nothing so I can take my baby to the park," she said and got into the truck.

"Lei baby I love you. I swear I love you and I love Deja. I want you, I want DJ. So, please just bear with me and let me work this out."

"No please Devon, don't do any favors for me. Go back and spend time with Michelle. That's what you want."

"Its work, that's it," he said, looking Leila in her eyes, lying.

"Yes, I'm sure you working hard to please someone other than your wife," Leila said and shut the door. Devon stood there and tapped on the window, but Leila cranked her truck and put it in gear to pull out. He stood there looking at her and she waved her hand, instructing him to step back. He hesitated, but he realized that he wouldn't get anywhere, so he stepped back.

Leila drove away telling herself not to cry, but the tears burned her eyes and she couldn't control it. She decided to go home instead. She was so upset because she confronted reality that she had to really move on. She and Devon were honestly over and he and Michelle was an item.

She took the baby and fed her and put her in her swing. She undressed and cleaned the makeup from her face. She was done and Devon knew that the gig was up because he was calling her cell phone every ten minutes. She looked at the mirror and the image of little petite sexy Michelle opening the door looking like a black Barbie doll made her angry. She sobbed and wished she hadn't changed. She wished her figure was still the figure she had six years ago when she and Devon got married.

She went downstairs and grabbed the ice cream out of the

freezer and got a spoon. She sat on the sofa and cried and ate the ice cream. She got up and she accidentally knocked her purse over and all of her belongings fell on the floor. She sat the ice cream on the coffee table to pick up her stuff. As she put her items back into her purse, she picked up Rayshon's card. She then looked at the ice cream and decided to give Rayshon a call.

VII

"Hi, this is Ray," he said when he answered.

"Hello Rayshon, this is Leila from the bookstore," she said nervously.

"Hey Leila, how's it going?"

"Okay I guess," she said and he could hear the sadness in her voice.

"What's wrong? You sound down."

"I'm fine, just had a bad day."

"I feel you. I've had one a time or two."

"Yeah, I've been having them a lot here lately."

"Don't sweat it. Things don't stay bad for long."

"I guess."

"So, I'm taking it you're finally calling to set up that session?"

"Yes, you are correct."

"That's great. When did you wanna start?"

"Well I don't know. How early or how late do you take appointments?"

"Well that depends on if you want to meet at the gym or at my loft?"

"What's the difference?"

"Well my mornings are done here at my loft and late evenings I sometimes meet at the gym. Time slots vary in cost because early, early and late, late is a higher rate and if you are not signing up for a gym membership you will have to come here anyway because to be honest all of my clients that I do see at the gym has a membership there."

"Okay, so what's the earliest and what's the latest?"

"The earliest is five a.m. and the latest is nine p.m. It depends on what works best for the client and what is open for scheduling."

"Wow, I didn't know it would be this complicated."

"Well really it isn't. We just have to get a schedule for you. Just keep in mind no Sundays. I am always off on Sundays."

"Wow, that is the best day for me," she said wishing Sundays were available.

"Well my apologies. I have to have at least one day off."

"It's okay. I just have to figure out how I can get time with my baby, you know?"

"You're a mom?"

"Yeah, I have a three month-old little girl."

"Oh, that's cool. What's her name?"

"Deja, she was born May fifteenth."

"Awesome. I bet your husband is proud."

"Yeah he's the proud daddy."

"Well how about you figure out a convenient time for you and your husband to set up an appointment and let me know. Then I'll see what schedule I can get you guys on."

"Well to be completely honest with you Rayshon, Devon will not be coming with me."

"Okay," he said, wondering why, but he didn't ask. "Just you coming is cool. Just let me know when you are ready."

"Okay, what about Tuesday? Can I meet with you on Tuesday morning? Renee usually opens on Tuesdays and I can come around eight o'clock in the morning to pick out some type of schedule I can do."

"Tuesday is good, but unfortunately eight is bad because I have an eight o'clock on Tuesday. Seven is early, but I'm free from seven 'til eight after my six o'clock. If not, I can't see you 'til two that afternoon."

"Okay, I guess I can come at seven because Renee needs to leave by two thirty on Tuesdays and I need to be at my store."

"Okay, seven it is," he said and they hung up. Ray was happy that she finally called. He was even happier that he didn't have to look at her husband's face. He was wondering what was going on with her marriage and why her man wouldn't be interested in working out with his wife. He went back to the football game and he could hardly concentrate. He was now thinking about Leila and he tried hard not to.

He picked up his phone, looked at the caller ID and saved her number in his phone so if something happened and she didn't show up he'd be able to call her. He went into the kitchen to make a snack and someone tapped on his door. He went to the door and it was a woman named Trisha that he absolutely didn't want to be bothered with.

One of his friends hooked him up with her, but it was whack. Her head was not on straight and he tried to be nice, but she just wasn't getting the picture. He reluctantly opened the door and planned on talking to her at the door and not inviting her in.

"Hey Trisha, what's up?" he asked, standing in front of the door.

"Hey Ray, we gotta talk."

"Okay what's up?" he asked, not inviting her in.

"Can I come in?" she asked and he paused for a second and then stepped aside to let her in. His momma taught him better than that.

"Look, I only got a few minutes because I have to head out soon," he said, lying to her. He didn't want to be bothered with this chick. She was cute and all, but she had no ambitions and she had that *'I'm waiting on a rich man to marry and take care of me'* mentality. Ray grew up with his mom and she was a strong single mother and if his momma didn't teach him anything else she always instilled in him *'God bless the child that got his own.'*

"So, what's going on?" he asked her after she took a seat.

"I didn't wanna stop by unannounced, but you haven't returned any of my calls."

"Well Trisha business is booming and I've been mad busy," he said, making an excuse. He was busy - yes, but not too busy to return a phone call.

"Well Ray, we have a problem," she said and he looked at her confused. What type of problem could they possibly have?

"We have a problem?" he asked sarcastically.

"Yes we do," she said stalling.

"Okay, are you gon' tell me what this problem is?"

"Yeah, but can I have a drink of water?"

"Sure," he said and went into the kitchen and got her a bottle of water from the fridge. He handed it to her and she opened it and almost drank the entire bottle and Ray sat there waiting for her to get to the point of why she was there. She finished her water and sat there for a few moments, not saying anything.

"Hey Trisha," he said and she jumped like he snapped her out of a trance.

"Oh yeah," she said and he was like '*this chick is nuts.*'

"Well I don't want you to be mad," she said, beating around the bush.

"Okay come on Trish, spit it out."

"I'm pregnant," she said and he didn't react.

"Okay, how is that my problem?"

"Because you're the father," she said and he couldn't believe she said it with a straight face.

"Well my dear, you may wanna check your calendar because I'm not the one."

"Yes you are."

"How do you figure?"

"Come on Ray, I'm not lying."

"Okay Trish, I know you would have liked for this to work, but it didn't okay? Now you can take your show on the road because you are not pregnant by me. Now I am not gonna argue with you, I'm just gonna ask you to leave and I'd like for you to not call me anymore."

"How you gon' act like you innocent Ray? I wouldn't be here if I wasn't absolutely positive it was yours."

"Okay, I can see you're a little loony or maybe you've been fucking around so much 'til you don't keep track of who you mess with because it is more likely for me to find a million dollars on the street than to be your baby's daddy."

"Ray you're such an asshole. I will see your coward ass in court!" she yelled and Ray was insulted and pissed.

"Listen Trisha, I didn't wanna go there, but you've forced me. I have to talk to you like the dumb ass you are being. Unless you can conceive in your jaws, that is not my baby. The night we made out, all we did was oral. Well let me take that back. All you did was oral. You were so messed up, you did your thang and I didn't even get to nut in you or anywhere near you because after three minutes of you damn near performing surgery on my man, I pulled you off. I calmed you down and I left you in bed by yourself. The next morning when you got up, you assumed that we got it on, but we didn't. I haven't returned your calls because it was a totally jacked up date. After you drank Long Island after Long Island, I was turned off," he said, looking at her, wondering where this girl came from.

"After I dropped you off the next day, I was hoping you remembered how you acted the night before and would be too embarrassed to call me, but when you called and called and called I knew you were not wrapped too tight," he said and wished he could have taken back that last statement.

"Listen Trisha, I'm sorry, but I am not the one," he said and she didn't have anything else to say. She looked at him and he could see how foolish she must have felt. She put the water bottle down on the coffee table and got up and left. Ray shook his head and laughed his ass off. He called his boy Mario and told him what went down. He was so tripped out about that scene; he laughed himself to sleep that night.

VIII

When Leila got to Ray's building, she was nervous. She was ten minutes early and she didn't want to wait in the truck. She got Deja and walked into his building and took the elevator to his floor. When she knocked, she heard his voice say, "Give me a minute." She stood there, waited a few moments and he opened the door.

"Hey Leila come on in and have a seat over here. I'm still with a client, so give me a few minutes," he said and she followed him and had a seat. She was a few minutes early so she didn't mind waiting.

He dashed back to the steps and ran up in a flash. Leila sat there and overheard them finishing up. When the session was over, they came down and Leila saw Christa. She was beautiful, Leila thought to herself and she felt embarrassed. She had on a two-piece workout suit and her stomach looked like she did a million sit ups a day. Leila felt intimidated and thought maybe it was a bad idea for her to be there.

"Hi I'm Christa," she said when she noticed Leila sitting by the desk.

"Hello I'm Leila."

"I see you are here to get rid of those pounds from the baby?" she said and Leila thought that was her nice way of saying you fat as hell, but she played it off.

"Well I guess you can say that," Leila said, not knowing how to respond. She was a plus size woman and looking at Christa, she felt like the ugly fat girl.

"Well you've come to the right place because he is magical," she said, like Ray was a miracle worker. "In no time you'll be in a two piece," Christa said and Leila wanted to slap her. It was obvious that Christa had never had a weight problem or a baby.

"Yeah I've heard," Leila said hoping she'd finish putting on her jacket and leave her alone.

"Well good luck on your weight loss journey and Ray, I will see you tomorrow," she said and finally made her exit. Ray closed the door and turned his attention to Leila.

"Good morning Miss Leila. I'm glad to see you and this is your little one?" he asked, turning the baby seat around to see Deja. She was awake and started laughing as soon as he started talking to her. "She is precious and beautiful, just like her momma," he said and Leila blushed.

"Thank you," she said, smiling.

"Yeah, I need to get down to business because two beautiful women in my place is too much pressure," he said and they laughed. They went over the schedule and Leila thought she'd start with Tuesdays and Thursdays. She chose eleven; that way the baby would be at daycare and Renee would be at the store. She was excited and anxious to get started. He told her to come twenty minutes early so they could go over nutrition and how to separate good carbs, from bad carbs.

They chatted 'til his eight o'clock arrived and Leila wanted to kill herself when she saw the next diva he had to train. Ray was fine - yes and the women coming in there had to be trying to get with him as a good as he looked and as fine as the two girls Leila saw; she felt like chopped liver. As good as Christa and Nina looked, she knew they didn't have to work hard to get or keep a man.

She wondered how many of his clients he was dating or sleeping with. Christa did say he was magical - how magical and magical at what? She wondered as he let her out. She waited for the elevator, wondering if she was really ready to come back. She didn't want to look like a fat fool in front of Ray, but it was too late; she had already signed her contract.

On Thursday, a couple days later, after Leila talked herself into actually showing up, she parked her Armada on his street. She had on sweats and an oversized tee shirt under her jacket. She looked at the underweight miniature woman that was coming down the hall on her way to Ray's loft and she wanted to turn back and go home. Where are these flat stomach, plumped ass youngsters coming from? Leila wondered.

"Hello," the woman said as she passed.

"Hi, how are you?" Leila asked with a smile.

"I'm fine," she said and Leila thought to herself, *'you got that right.'* She got to Ray's door and tapped a couple of times and he opened the door.

"Hey Leila, good to see you," Ray said, looking even more sexy than he did the other day. He had on a black tank and his shoulders looked good enough to eat, she thought to herself.

"Hey, I hope I'm not too early."

"No you are fine. Come on in and let me get your folder," he said, walking over to his office area. He pulled out a folder and started getting a couple blank forms that looked like a profile, but Leila wasn't sure. She was happy to see that his business was legit and he wasn't running some type of ghetto fabulous establishment.

"Okay before we get started today I wanna tape you and get your weight."

"Huh - is this standard?"

"Yes my dear, I'm afraid it is. How else will we know if we are making progress?" he asked with a smile.

"I don't know Ray, maybe this was a bad idea," she said reluctant.

"Listen Leila, you don't have to feel embarrassed or uncomfortable with me. I've seen it all. Your weight and your size are fine. I know why you're here, so come on relax," he said, trying to make her feel relaxed. "I'm here to help you get started on a workout regiment. That is it, after you learn the tools to be healthier; you will no longer need me. So come on, let me get your measurements so we can get started," he said and she was hesitant, but she stood up to allow him to tape her.

He could still see the fear of stepping onto the scale in her eyes, so he did the, '*I know your weight*' thing because he pretty much could guess a person's weight just by looking at them.

"Hey I betcha I can tell you how much you weigh and if I'm wrong you don't have to get on the scale today, but if I can at least guess within five pounds of what you weigh, you have to tell me."

"What?" she asked smiling.

"I'm going to turn my head and you get on the scale and if the number on that scale is within five pounds of what I guessed, you have to tell me today. If I'm wrong, you don't have to tell me 'til you are ready to tell me."

"Okay Mr. Johnson, what's your guess?" she asked, up for the challenge.

"Um, let me see, step back a little. You are 5' 5", so I'd say two seventeen," he said and she wondered why he said such a high number; she knew she couldn't be over two hundred pounds.

"Two seventeen, you know you're wrong," she said with attitude.

"Yep, I say two seventeen and you my dear must have not weighed yourself in awhile," he said, looking at her with a straight face. Now Leila was determined to prove a point.

"Okay mister turn around," she said and he did. She stepped onto the scale and the digital numbers stopped on two twenty one and she almost hit the floor. She could not believe that he was within five pounds for one and she didn't realize she weighed that much.

"Okay, okay - you're right. I guess you do know your stuff."

"Was I right?"

"No, it was two twenty one," she said and sat down in the chair. Her face went from sad to sadder.

"Hey Leila, don't look so disappointed. You will be alright; you just have to be patient and you will see," he said, trying to make her feel better, but she didn't.

"Well that is easy for you to say. Now I feel like I have to stop eating for the rest of my life."

"No, that will only make it worse. Here is a list of things you can have a whole lot of and this other list are the things I want you to stay away from," he said, giving her the list and she looked over it.

"Rice, I can't eat rice?" she asked disappointed because she loved Chinese food.

"You can, but stay away from white rice. Brown rice is okay, but not much of it."

"And potatoes and sour cream? Come on, I feel like I'm going on punishment."

"Leila come on, some of these things are okay in moderation, but in order to jump start your metabolism you are going to have to make changes to your diet."

"Damn, why did I have to wait 'til thirty to gain weight? I've never had an issue with my weight; for years I maintained a ten and now I can't shop in the mall."

"Leila, don't get discouraged before you try it. This is the beginning and it will take you at least twenty one days before your

48

body and your appetite will adjust to this, but you have to be here to give it one hundred and ten percent or else you are wasting my time and your money."

"I know Ray, I'm ready."

"That's what I wanted to hear. You can do this."

"Yeah I know. It isn't gonna be easy, but I'm ready."

"Okay well let's go up so we can get started," he said and she followed him up the steps. "Today we are gonna start with the basics and you will be a little sore tomorrow, but please don't let that stop you from coming back. It will get easier as your muscles get used to the change, so give it time."

"Okay," she said, listening carefully to everything he said.

"We are going to start with stretching and if anything hurts or if you can't do something, let me know," he said gently, making Leila feel more relaxed and comfortable. It felt kind of weird to her, but slowly she got more into it. When the session was over, she was happy she decided to sign up. She also knew she was going to have to get her hair braided because the little that they had done had her sweating like a pig.

He gave her a bottle of water and made sure she was feeling okay. She smiled and assured him that everything was cool. He walked her to the door and he asked her again.

"So, was it fun?"

"Yes it was. Hard, but for the most part fun."

"That is what I like to hear."

"And thanks so much for being so patient with me, because there were moments where I know I looked stupid," she said and they laughed.

"You did fine; just keep in mind that things don't happen overnight. You have to be patient and stick to it."

"I plan to."

"Good then I'll see you on Tuesday and try to go by that diet plan over the weekend. Don't let this part be a waste," he said and smiled.

"I will and thanks again."

"It was my pleasure," he said and she walked away. She smiled all the way to her truck. She wondered if he was always that pleasant and treated folks like he treated her. That was completely opposite of what she expected from him. She honestly did judge him and make him out to be an egotistical jerk and he was far from it.

She wondered if he had a woman and quickly tried to stop herself from going there. He was fine - yes, but no way was she beautiful enough for him to want her. If Devon didn't want her, for sure Rayshon - fine to the bone, wouldn't think twice about her, not when he had opportunities to be in contact with women like Christa and that woman she saw earlier in the hall.

She drove back to the bookstore with fantasies of Rayshon. She wished she looked like she looked when she was in college. You couldn't tell her she wasn't fine back then. She had the body and the brains and she remembered how crazy Devon was about her. She glanced at herself in the mirror and thought to herself how any man would ever want her like that again, especially not Rayshon. The only solution she could come up with as to why he treated her so kindly was he wanted her check to clear.

He was pretty pricy, but if he could make her look like one of his other trainees, she'd give him a million bucks. She got back to the bookstore and tried to get Rayshon out of her mind, but as soon as she walked in, she spent the entire afternoon talking to Renee about him. She knew that she'd never have a man like him in this lifetime, but she enjoyed fantasizing about it.

IX

Leila was getting into her truck when her cell phone rang. She looked at the LCD screen and it was Devon. She got in and settled into her seat before she answered.

"Yes Devon, I am on my way," she told him because she had to pick up the baby from him.

"Good, because we need to talk," he said, sounding sad on the phone.

"What is it? Is Deja okay?" she asked, concerned.

"DJ is fine, that isn't what I want to discuss with you Lei."

"What is it Devon? You sound so serious."

"Well I got the divorce papers today," he said and it made Leila nervous. Her stomach instantly got butterflies. She knew he'd be getting them soon, but she wasn't ready to discuss it with him.

"Okay, I will be there in about thirty minutes," she said and ended the phone call. She smiled because she was relieved, but at the same time, she was a bit nervous about seeing him face to face. She rehearsed the speech that she had planned to say to him when the time had come for her to follow through with her plans to finally give him what he threatened to give her for months.

When she got to his place, she parked in the guest-parking stall and opened the visor to check herself in the mirror. She had gotten her hair done earlier that day and she wanted to make sure she still looked good. She powdered her face with her sponge and reapplied her lip-gloss. She checked her teeth to make sure there was no food stuck in-between them. She popped a mint into her mouth and cut off the engine.

When she got up to his door, she lifted her arm to knock, but Devon opened the door before she could.

"Come on in," he said and walked away quickly. He went into the kitchen and took a pan off the stove. She went over to her baby, who was in her playpen.

"Hey girlfriend, how ya doing baby girl?" she asked, talking to her baby. She was getting so big and her mommy was getting so small. Well at least dropping her pounds at a rapid, but healthy rate. She was looking good and was down by thirty-five pounds since she started and it showed and she felt good.

"So Lei, you are looking good," Devon said, coming up behind her.

"Thanks," she said and put the baby back down. She sat on the sofa and waited for Devon to get started with their discussion.

"So how are things at the store?" he asked, making small talk.

"Things are good. And at the company?" she asked, not really caring, just being courteous. Every since Michelle has been a factor and she works at the same company, Leila made it a point not to bring up his job.

"Things are going really good."

"That's good to hear Devon," she said, looking at him. She didn't want to ask, but she had to get this conversation on the road. "So what did you wanna talk about Devon?"

"Do you want a drink?" he asked.

"You know I'm still nursing," she said, looking at him like he was slow.

"Yeah, yeah, that's right. I didn't know, maybe you had some milk pumped. I didn't think Lei. I can get you some water or juice," he offered.

"No Devon, I'm fine. I just can't stay too much longer. I got to go by the store and do the books."

"Well I guess I should get straight to the point huh?"

"Yeah that would be a good idea."

"Lei why are you doing this?" he asked her, looking pathetic.

"Come on Devon, you've been telling me every other month that you want a divorce. Now that I go out to finally give you what you said you wanted, you ask me why."

"Lei I changed my mind okay? I love you and DJ and I know I've made a huge mistake and I'm willing to drop everything right now if you just give me another chance. I don't want the divorce. I want you, I want Deja. Please, I want to come home," he said and he looked genuine, but Leila wasn't buying it. She wasn't going to let him get back into her life and hurt her all over again.

She had moved on and had a fresh start and he wasn't about to talk her into giving him another chance to hurt her. She gave him opportunity after opportunity to come home and now her head was clear and she was ready to let go.

"Devon please, I can't go there with you. Why can't you just get this over with? You know you don't wanna be with me. You just don't want me to be with someone else. It is perfectly fine for you to be with Michelle, but I can't have freedom to get on with my life," she asked standing.

"Is that why you are divorcing me - because of Michelle? You are going through with the divorce because you think I'm with Michelle?"

"No Devon, I'm not jealous of that little lying trick. I could care less about Michelle. I just want a life too Devon. You have this fabulous single life where you are having parties, dating and who knows what and all I've done is sit around and wonder if you will come back to me. I'm tired of wondering if this will be the day or will it be tomorrow or will he ever. I sat around for a long time waiting and waiting."

"You don't have to wait on me Lei. I'm right here and I'm ready now to start over. I promise that I am ready to love you like you deserve to be loved. Like I should have been doing for the longest time and I know I messed up Lei. I am not saying that I was the stand up dude who always did right by you. Can't you just forgive me and let the past go?" he asked, pleading. He moved closer to her and she backed away making sure she kept her distance because she wasn't completely over Devon.

"Devon I have forgiven you," she said, moving across the room. "I don't hate you, I just can't trust you. When I was pregnant, you walked out on me. You left me alone and by myself. I cried so much and prayed that you'd come to your senses and come home. You abandoned me when I needed you the most because you were so disgusted because I changed. You criticized me and treated me like I was this burden and you looked at me like I was nobody," she said, trying not to cry. Her mind went back to the times when she was alone and pregnant without her husband. How he'd passed through like she was just his baby's momma, with no regard to her feelings. "So what's so different now Devon? Why do you want me now?"

"I've always wanted you Lei. I've loved you since the first day I met you. I just had a stupid moment. I went through this horrible selfish phase and I know I treated you bad Lei and I'm so sorry, baby please. I don't want this divorce. I want you," he said, walking over to her and he put his arms around her waist.

"Stop it Devon please – stop, just stop it, okay?" she said and walked away from his embrace.

"Lei come here baby. Look at me please, come on, look at me," he said, following behind her.

"No Devon, I gotta go okay? Get DJ's things. I gotta go," she said, moving to get the baby. Deja was laughing and playing, having a good time by herself.

"No Lei, I can't let you walk out. I don't want this. I don't want this divorce. I won't give you a divorce," he said, raising his voice. Leila was touched and wanted to turn to him to say *"Okay,"* but she couldn't. She put the baby back down and went into the bathroom without saying another word to him. She shut the door and fought the tears. She loved Devon, but she was over the heartache and drama. She just wished he would have said something a long time ago. She wished he wanted their marriage back when she was pregnant, when she would have taken him back in a heartbeat.

Now things were so different and as much as she hated her situation, it was what it was. She didn't want to be the bad guy like he was making her out to be. She only granted him his wish. So many months he threw the word *"divorce"* in her face. Time after time, she had asked him to come home and start over. Too many times, she begged him to come home and make their marriage work, but he walked around doing his own thing and it was time for her to do the same.

She wiped her face and got herself together. She wasn't going to give in to him. She wasn't going to let him win. She was ready to end it and he wasn't going to change her mind. She opened the door and went back into the living room. Devon was sitting on the sofa with the baby and she paused in her tracks at the sight of them together. Deja was laughing and making happy baby sounds as her daddy talked her. Leila stood there and took it in for a moment and she then jerked herself away from the thought of them being a happy family again.

"You have her things Devon? I gotta go," she said, picking up the baby's bottle from the playpen. Devon got up and handed her to Leila and Deja started to cry.

Mommy is ready to go," she said and Deja continued to cry for her daddy.

"Here…, give her to me for a moment," he said, trying to take her out of Leila's arms.

"No Devon, please go and get her stuff; she'll be fine," Leila said with resistance.

"Lei come on, I'm not going to let her cry like this," he said, still trying to get her out of Leila's arms.

"Okay here take her," she said, giving in. "Where is her bag?" she asked looking around.

"In the bedroom," he said and Leila went into his room to get her baby's things. When she opened the door, his room was immaculately clean and his big bed was made. She took her focus off the bed and looked around for Deja's bag. She spotted it by the nightstand and she saw his cell phone. The light was flashing and she couldn't resist picking it up. She hit the button to light up the screen and it had six missed calls and the screen said Michelle.

She wondered how he was planning on getting back with her when Michelle was still in his life. She put the phone down and walked out. She knew then that he was full of shit because he wanted to play her when he still had something going on with Michelle, but she wasn't going to fall for that. She was confident and she was in no mood to be crying over Devon again.

"Okay Deja we gotta go," she said again and Deja refused to go along with the program. She started to cut up again. "What is it momma, why are you being a bad girl?" Leila asked.

"Because she doesn't want to leave her daddy, that's what's wrong, she wants to stay."

"Well I have stuff to do Devon," she said impatiently.

"Look she can stay here. You go do what you gotta do."

"Then what, come all the way back over here?" she asked, looking at him like that was definitely a bad idea.

"No call me when you are on your way home and I'll bring her."

"No Devon, that is too much. I can take her now. She is just gonna have to behave," Leila said, putting her foot down.

"No Lei, I'm not doing anything tonight and I don't mind keeping my angel. So go and I'll bring her home."

"Are you sure?"

"Yes I'm sure."

"Okay," she said and kissed her baby. "Mommy will see you later sweetie pie," she said and grabbed her purse. Devon was standing like he was waiting for a kiss too.

"Lei I'll see you later and we will continue where we left off."

"There is nothing more to discuss," she said, putting on her coat.

"Oh there is," he said and Leila opened the door to leave.

"Whatever, I'll see you and Deja later," she said and shut the door.

X

"So when are you gonna tell her?" Mario asked Ray.

"Tell who what?"

"Come on now Ray, you have been my boy since forever and I know that you are digging her."

"Man you don't know what you are talking about. For one, that woman is married. For two, she is a client and three…, well there's no three, but I'm not feeling her."

"Damn Ray, why do you always act like you are this cool cat, so laid back and not into these females? You act like it's impossible for you to dig a woman that is one of your so-called clients. Personally, I never figured it to be Leila; I always thought you'd be trying to get with one of them model chicks, but I see that you do like the heavy ones," he said jokingly.

"Hey man, watch your mouth. You know I don't talk about people that way. We all can't be the same size and shape and you know I don't dog people like that."

"Man you act like you don't look at overweight women or even men and think that they look disgusting," Mario said, laughing.

"No I don't, because I am educated to know that obesity is a disease you insensitive jerk. If I wanted to make fun of overweight people or treat them like an outcast, I would have never gone into this line of business dumb ass."

"Chill out man, I'm just talking shit. The point is, you need to be honest and tell that woman you are feeling her. I can tell because you go to the bookstore more times than you go to the bathroom," he said and they laughed.

"Man gon' with that," Ray said, pushing his shoulder.

"I'm serious dude. You talk about her all the damn time."

"I don't - you bring her up more than I do. You must want her," he said.

"Dawg please, you know I don't bring that woman up. I don't know her like that, but every time we get together all you do is find a way to bring her up. You be like, man Leila put me onto this book or man, Leila told me about this or in our last session Leila told me that so and so that. So, if you can't be honest with her at least tell me the truth. You digging her aren't you?" he asked and Ray paused. He hesitated and decided to stick to his story.

"Man she is a client. I don't mix business with pleasure."

"Yeah that is why yo' ass is celibate now, because you only do business and no pleasure."

"Man you know I have a social life. I mean, not all my time is business. I'm out with you tonight aren't I?" he asked and took a sip of is Hennessey.

"Yes that is because I wasn't gonna take no for an answer this time. I mean, since you and Katrina broke up you different."

"See there you go. Why you have to go there? When I am not thinking about that woman and my mind is completely rested, you go there," he said, taking a gulp of his drink and shaking his head. "Can I get another one?" he asked the bartender.

"Ray man my bad. I was only saying dude, you haven't had a woman in what, six or seven years? When did y'all break up again – '03, '04?" Mario asked and Ray didn't find him amusing at all.

"Look man it was '03 and I've had women since then," he said and paid the bartender after he put his drink down in front of him.

"Yes, you have had some ass, but a woman? Name one woman you went out with for more than a month since Katrina?" he asked and Ray said nothing. He had to think and no one came to mind. "See, now what? I told you," Mario said and took a swallow of his beer.

"Ramona - ha, Ramona man," he said, looking at him like now what.

"Oh yeah Ramona, what - y'all kick it for what - three months? Wow that was deep."

"Damn man, why you sweatin' me?"

"Because I think you'd be a happier man if you'd be honest and tell that woman that you like her. I mean, what's the worst can happen?"

"She could ruin my business. I could regret it for the rest of my life. Let's see, Mario, how about me losing a client? She is doing so well and if I hurt her and go messing with our professional relationship, she may fall back into that rut."

"What rut?"

"Look she and her husband had some issues okay? And she was hurt by him and I don't want to get involved with her and things don't work. I mean, Leila is a very special lady. She is smart and vibrant. She has come out of the shell she was in and her confidence is higher than it was the day I met her at the bookstore," he said, taking another sip.

"So, what you are saying is you are not gonna get involved with this woman based on the fact that you will hurt her?"

"No I won't hurt her," he said defensively.

"So, what is your problem? I mean, it is obvious that you dig this woman and from what you've told me in our hundreds of conversations, she is now divorcing him and has decided to move on with her life, so the ex is not a factor - what are you - my friend - afraid of?" he asked and Ray was quiet for a moment. It's like he had to think of another excuse to keep from sharing his feelings with Leila.

"Look man, I'm not afraid okay? I just think it's not the right time to pursue Leila."

"Okay then, when do you think it will be the right time? After she goes off and meets some other dude? Oh yes, she is a thick sista, but she is also fine and you sitting up here chilling and backing up. One day she is gonna come to one of them little sessions and tell you about some guy named Dexter Saint Cock and you gon' wish you hadda stepped up to the plate," he said and it made Ray think a moment. What if he were right? Yes, Leila is very pretty and a man with eyes would be foolish to look past her.

After that comment, Ray's mood changed and suddenly he was not in the mood to be out at their spot anymore. He paid for his last drink and told Mario, after he finished he would be heading out. He got up and went to the bathroom and when he came back, there were two fine sista's sitting at the bar near his stool. He hesitated to approach because he saw that Mario had already engaged in conversation with them.

He took his seat, said hello and exchanged introductions with them. He was set to depart, but Mario practically begged him to stay for another round and he agreed. After a little conversation, he found out that Karen, the one sitting close to him, was in nursing school and worked at a hospital nearby. He couldn't make out too much of what Leslie was saying because of the music, but he nodded and was attentive to the conversation.

Karen was pretty - yes, with bright skin tone and wavy hair that she wore down and it hung a little past her shoulders. Although she was sitting, Ray could determine she was about five feet and maybe one hundred and fifteen pounds and her friend Leslie, also fair complexioned, was about five feet seven and maybe about one hundred forty pounds and they were very attractive.

Karen flirted with Ray, but his mind was not there. It was on Leila. He wondered what she was doing and where she was. Could she have been with another man out on a date or at dinner? Could she be in another man's arms? He was trying to focus on the conversation with Karen, but it was difficult for him to do.

"So, you are a personal trainer?" Karen asked.

"Yes, that is what I do," he responded with a fake smile. He didn't want to be rude to her and since her friend had found her way to the stool on the other side of Mario, he felt obligated to talk to her.

"So, you think you can whip my body into shape?" she asked, flirting heavily and he knew he had to end the conversation quick before she asked him about setting up an appointment.

"Well it looks like you have that under control," he said, implying that she didn't need his services.

"Yeah, I do what I can, but I know with a little training I could always look better," she said, giving him a sexy smile.

"Yeah, there is always room for improvement," he said, looking away. He was trying hard not to be cold to her; he just couldn't take his mind off what Mario said about Leila getting with another dude.

"Yes there is, so do you think I can get a session?" she asked, leaning over, giving him a peep at her cleavage.

"Well I'd have to see about getting you on my books," he said and sipped his drink. He tried to move his eyes from her cleavage, but it was difficult because she had a low cut top on that exposed her perfectly round mounds and she looked good.

"How about you do that," she said and smiled.

"Oh yes, I will," he said, making her feel like a sexy woman. She was attractive and Ray made it a habit to always make a woman feel like a woman and she was definitely a woman that had it going on.

"Listen, I gotta run because I have another spot that I promised my sister I would hit and if I don't show you know how that goes," he said, lying.

"So soon?" she asked, disappointed.

"Yeah it's like her man's birthday or some shit and I promised I'd be there," he said, hating to lie, but he had to bounce. "Here is my card and you can call me to set up that appointment," he said, getting up and putting on his leather jacket.

"Ray man, you out?" Mario asked when he saw him get up.

"Yeah man, you know I got to go by Rhonda's; it's Kenny's birthday," he said, acting like he had told him something about it earlier.

"Oh yeah man, I almost forgot," he said, going along with Ray. He didn't know a damn thing about it being Kenny's birthday. "Excuse me Leslie, I'm gonna walk my boy out."

"Okay, I'll be right here waiting," she said, giving him a sexy smile. He turned and walked Ray out the door.

"Thanks man for not busting a brother out," he told Mario when they got outside.

"No problem, I know what's up," he said.

"Well you my friend, don't go getting into any trouble because last I heard you and your woman was on the road to success."

"I know my friend. I'm gonna talk a little shit and hang out and I am gonna be out shortly trust," he said and they shook.

"You betta, because yo' woman will have your ass on the six o'clock news."

"True - True. Get home safe."

"You too dawg," Ray said and headed toward his Tahoe.

"Yo," Mario yelled out to him.

"What's up?"

"Talk to the woman. Be real," Mario said.

"Soon man, soon," he responded and walked away. He got home and it was still early, not even eleven o'clock. He decided to get on the treadmill to think. After running two miles, it still was not even midnight, so he showered and put on some sweats. He looked over at his work area and walked over and turned on the light. He looked through his file cabinet and took out Leila's file. He opened it and looked at her picture that he had taken the first day she started and he smiled because there was already a difference in the way she looked.

Not saying he didn't like her before or he didn't find her attractive then, he was just proud of her success. She was doing what she was supposed to do and it showed. He put her file away and wondered if it would be rude to call her. He looked over at the clock and it read eleven forty and he decided it would be rude to call her that late at night. He turned out the light on his desk and went into the living room and turned on the television. After an hour of nothing, he decided to turn in.

He got in the bed and as soon as he shut his eyes, his cell phone rang. He looked at the clock and thought maybe it was Mario calling at a quarter 'til one, but when he looked at the ID, he didn't recognize the number.

"Hello," he said in his deep and sexy tone.

"Hey are you still out?" the voice on the other end asked.

"Who is this?" he asked, sitting up in his bed.

"This is Karen, I was calling to see if you were able to fit me in your schedule?" she asked. He knew what time it was.

"Well actually, when are you available?" he asked, going along with her. It was damn near one o'clock in the morning, he was still a man and she was fine.

"I can be available in about thirty minutes. Where are you located?" she asked.

"I see you are ready to burn some calories?" he asked.

"Oh yes I am, how about you?" she asked.

"I could use a good workout before I go to sleep," he said, standing and moving over to his nightstand. He opened it to check his supply of condoms. He was good and he knew what was about to go down. He gave her directions and hung up. He went into the bathroom and brushed his teeth again. He turned on some soft music and waited for her to get to his place. He lit a few candles to set the mood in his loft and before he could make a mental note not to think about Leila, she knocked on the door.

He opened the door and little miss Karen was standing in the doorway. He invited her in and took her coat. They didn't talk much before he had her in his bed. She was a wildcat in bed and he did enjoy the night that they shared together. He fell right to sleep and dreamed of him and Leila. He dreamed of her being with him in his kitchen, cooking a meal, drinking wine and laughing with each other. He dreamt of touching her face and caressing her cheek. He was happy in his dream just to enjoy her smiles and to hear her laughter.

The next morning when he woke, he remembered the exciting night he had shared with Karen. She was cool and he enjoyed her, but she wasn't Leila. He didn't wake her when he eased out of the bed to go to the bathroom. He went into the kitchen, poured himself a glass of orange juice and opened the door to retrieve his Sunday's paper. He glanced at the clock and it was only eight a.m.

He sat at the island in his kitchen and read the paper and enjoyed his juice. After an hour, he went back into his bedroom and Karen was still asleep. He was a gentleman and he didn't wake her. He pulled the door up behind him and pulled all the curtains in his loft open to expose the downtown Chicago view. It was glorious and he was pleased with his place. He turned on the music and proceeded to do some cleaning, like he always did on Sundays.

His place was never a mess, but he made it a point to maintain the dust and keep it spotless. It was not only his home, but it was where he did business. After he dusted and swept, he organized the office area. By the time he was done, it was after eleven a.m. and Karen had not budged. He didn't want to be an asshole, but she had to go, because he had to get water and energy bars to stock up for the week and he was not in the habit of leaving strange women at his place.

"Hey Karen wake up," he whispered in her ear and she grunted and wiped her eyes.

"What time is it?"

"Eleven thirty," he said and she sat up in the bed.

"Damn, I'm sorry. I don't know why I slept so late," she said, getting up and looking around for her belongings. He had put her things on the chair neatly.

"It's cool. There is a toothbrush and fresh towels in the bathroom for you," he said, opening the drapes in his room, exposing yet another beautiful view. She stood and her little petite body was perfect. No stretch marks and her breasts were still standing tall. He looked at her as she walked to the bathroom without grabbing anything to cover up with. Karen was definitely not shy.

"Thank you," she yelled from the bathroom.

"No problem," he said and went back into the living room area.

"This is a nice place," she said, coming out of the bedroom completely dressed.

"Thank you," he said, placing a glass of orange juice and a bagel on the island in front of her. He removed the frying pan from the stovetop and put her eggs on the plate with the bagel and gave her a little bowl of fresh fruit.

"Wow, you didn't have to do this Ray," she said, sitting at the island.

"It's no hassle. My momma always told me: if you have someone over, always make them feel welcome."

"Well your momma did a good job raising you with manners. Men are usually cold after a night of sex. Have your clothes on the porch the next morning," she said and chuckled.

"Well my dear, maybe you should choose your sex partners a little more carefully," he said and put the pan in the sink.

"I'm working on that," she said in an annoyed tone.

"Oh I'm sorry, that was a joke. I didn't mean that to be offensive," he said, correcting himself. He wasn't trying to be rude or disrespectful.

"It's cool. I'm okay," she said and he was relieved. She ate her food and he took her plate and placed it in the sink. "So, what's up there?" she asked, pointing to the gym area.

"Oh, there is where I do my sessions."

"Can I see?" she asked.

"Sure," he said and took her up.

"So, what's your story Mr. Ray, are you single?"

"Yep,"

"Why is that?" she asked, sitting on the workbench.

"Because I work a lot and I make it my business not to date my clients and since most of the women I come into contact with are clients - leaves little room for romance."

"Okay, well since you live by that rule, I don't want to become a client," she said and moved closer to him.

"Oh, so you don't want to enhance this body?" he asked while he touched her ass.

"No, I'd rather burn calories with you the way we did last night," she said and they kissed.

"Oh, that is not a bad idea," he said and removed her shirt. Before he could stop the presses, his mouth was sucking on her nipple. She stroked his man and he caressed her back. He picked her up and she wrapped her legs around his waist. They kissed and he thought about his condoms being downstairs, so he carried her down the steps and took her into his bedroom.

After they went at it again, they kissed each other goodbye and he told her he'd call her. He showered and dressed to go out to do his errands. When he got back to his loft, he changed his sheets and finished cleaning his bedroom and bathroom. He sat on the sofa to read a book that he had gotten from the bookstore a few days ago and the thoughts of Leila returned to his mind. He finished out his day without calling Karen because his focus had gone back to the woman he wanted and it was not Karen.

XI

Leila avoided Devon all weekend. When he brought Deja home Sunday, he tried to stick around to talk, but Leila pretended she was on her way out when he got there and told him she would call him when she got home, but she never did. All Sunday evening he called and called and she refused to answer. He showed up at the bookstore yesterday and she told him that she just needed time to think and he finally went with that answer and cut her some slack. She was confused and unsure on what to do next. She cared for Devon, but she didn't trust him.

She wondered if she let him back home how long would that last. Would she have to worry about him messing around with that five pound, twelve ounce little trick named Michelle? If she gained any of her weight back, would he trip out again and dog her? If she got pregnant again, would he pull another disappearing act? She thought about all these things. Why did she have to go through this? Why couldn't he just sign the papers and call it a day?

She rode to Ray's loft with heavy thoughts of her situation. She thought about canceling her appointment, but she didn't want to break her routine. The way she was feeling, she knew that if she cancelled that would lead her to ice cream and cookies on the couch. She had come too far to still allow Devon to control her life. She was finally conquering things on her own, in her own way and she was determined not to let her situation with the divorce set her back.

When she got to Ray's, she got off the elevator and coming down the hall was the one and only Christa. She was looking good, as she always did, but Leila was in no mood for her smart-ass mouth.

"Leila, how nice to see you," she said with her fake ass smile.

"Nice to see you," Leila returned.

"Ooh girl, you might have to give him a minute because he worked me over real good today," she said, sounding like a desperate tramp.

"Oh, I'm sure Ray will be alright; he has a way of doing the same for all of us," she snapped back. She wanted Christa to know she was no more special to Ray than she was and just like she got her money's worth so did she.

"I see. Well you enjoy. Too bad he sees you after he sees me," she said, walking to the elevator.

"No, actually it's a good thing because all you do is get him warmed up for me. Enjoy your day hun," Leila said and Christa didn't have anything to come back with. She stormed down hall and pressed the elevator button insanely. No matter how much she tried, she still could not get Ray to give in to her and the thought of a fat girl getting the man she wanted pissed her off.

Leila tapped on the door and she heard Ray tell her to come on in. She pushed the door open and he was not in the living room. She took off her coat and put it on the coat rack by the door and went upstairs. She was used to coming and she knew what to do to get started. She stretched and wondered what was keeping him. She got onto the treadmill and started her twenty-minute warm up. When he finally came up, she was already ten minutes into her walk.

He barely looked at her and she wondered what was bothering him. He apologized for keeping her waiting and he waited for her to be done with her walk. When she was done, she looked at him and he was looking good. He looked as if his haircut was just done and he smelled wonderful. He looked as if he had not had a session with Christa and when he spoke, she could smell the freshness of his breath. Not that he stunk before, but he was extra fresh, what we would call funky fresh that day.

Normally they laughed and talked during their session, but that day was different. He was kind of quiet and she didn't know why. She was normally a chatterbox, but since she had issues with Devon she really was at a loss for words herself, so things were oddly strange. When the session was over, instead of her hanging around chatting with him like they normally did, she left.

She drove back to the store, wondering if something did finally go down with him and Christa. Maybe that's what was keeping him. He had to shower and freshen up so she wouldn't smell the sex smell on him, she thought to herself. She didn't know why but it made her jealous. "That skinny bitch," she said out loud to herself as she drove back. "Monique is right; they are evil," she said and drove along. "First Michelle, now Christa; they think they can just have all the men," she said, talking to herself.

When she got back to the store, Renee was there and things were a bit busy. Leila didn't hesitate to help her to take care of the customers. After the crowd was clear, Leila took her things into the back. She looked up and noticed Renee standing in the doorway.

"What," Leila asked.

"You gon' take him back aren't you?" she asked, sounding disappointed.

"I don't know Renee," she said, taking off her boots and putting on her comfy shoes.

"Lei don't let him trick you. You have come so far," she said out of concern.

"Well you know what Renee? That is easy for you to say. You have a man," Leila snapped.

"Excuse me?" Renee said, shocked.

"Yes Renee, I said it. You have a man. You walk around here and you keep trying to convince me why I shouldn't give my husband another chance, when you go home to your husband every damn night. Look at me Renee; I'm not a size six like you. Men are not beating down my door. It is so easy for you to walk down the street and guys are trying to get with you. When you and I are together, guys treat me like I'm invisible. I have one man that is really trying to be with me and I don't know if I will ever have a man at least as half as fine as Devon to ever approach me and you keep trying to tell me to just forget him and let him go. News flash Renee; I am lonely and I am horny as hell and as much as Devon has done me wrong, I feel like taking him back so I can have someone to want me again," she said, venting all of her emotions. Renee was angry, but she understood.

"Look Lei, I am your friend and I am not looking down on you. I know what damage Devon has done. I have been there with you since the day he walked out and I have watched you suffer and cry so many times over him. I want what you want for you. I want whatever you decide for you that suits you best and if that is with Devon, so be it, but I just see a new woman. You are beautiful Lei and if a man can look over you and not see that, then he has the problem. Don't settle for Devon for the sake of not being alone because if he hurts you or does what he did again, you are going to hate yourself for allowing him to come back and that is not what I want for you. You are my friend and I love you and you deserve to be happy. The right man will come along Lei and you will not have to be lonely because you do deserve a good man in your life, but be honest, do you really want Devon back?"

"Renee you don't understand. It's more to it than that. We have a child...," she tried to say and Renee stopped her before she could come up with a million excuses.

"No Lei, no. That is not what I asked you. Do you want Devon back?" she asked again and the tears began to fall from Leila's eyes. She couldn't answered that and be honest with her friend.

"Renee I don't know right now. I just don't know," she said, not saying no. She didn't want Devon back, but to say no would be premature and she didn't want to be the one to eat her words if she and he got back together.

"Well take your time and I promise whatever you decide I will support you and always be here for you," she said and they hugged. They were in the back office 'til they heard the bell of the door. Renee went out to take care of the customer and she gave Leila a few moments to be alone.

After they closed, Leila went down the street to pick up Deja and she saw Devon's car. Oh Lord, she thought to herself. She got out and when she went inside, there he was signing Deja out.

"You didn't tell me you were coming to pick the baby up today Devon and you know the rules," she told him.

"I know, I know, that is why I was going to wait here for you. I didn't know if you picked her up yet. I thought I'd take my two girls out to dinner."

"Aw Devon, I'm so tired," she tried to say.

"Shhhh, come on Lei. Come to dinner with me," he said and she didn't resist.

"Okay Devon, okay," she said, not putting up a fight. She knew if she didn't he'd hound her and she was hungry.

She followed him and the baby to a nearby restaurant. They got out and went inside. They ordered and ate and Leila enjoyed being out with Devon. She and he hadn't been out in so long, it seemed strange. Before dinner was done, Deja was sleeping in her seat. They paid and Devon offered to follow them home. Things were going well so Leila didn't refuse him. When they got home, he helped her and the baby inside and he stayed 'til after Leila put the baby down. She showered and he hung around.

When she came down the stairs, he had dozed off on the sofa. She leaned over to wake him and when she touched him, he grabbed her arm.

"Oh, Lei I'm sorry."

"It's okay…, um, it's getting late Devon and you should go."

"Can I stay?" he asked and he seemed so loving and honest.

"No Devon, not yet. I'm not ready," she said and he rose up and kissed her. Her body went limp in his arms and her nipples hardened. She was trying to resist him, but she couldn't. She wanted him, she wanted to be loved and touched and she wanted him to do her body the way he used to. They were on the sofa making out and she moaned and panted from his kisses and his touch.

"I want you Lei," he whispered softly as he sucked on her neck and licked her breast. She was still full of milk, so he tried to refrain from sucking, but after a few moments, he couldn't resist and that turned Leila on. Her soft spot released a flow of sexual fluids and she wanted her husband.

"Come on Devon, let's go upstairs," she whispered.

"Okay," he said, anxious to feel his wife again. She went up before him and he made sure the door was locked and he set the alarm. He smiled because he knew he was there for the night. He took his cell phone out of his pocket along with his keys and he put them on the coffee table. He turned off the lights and went upstairs. Leila was in bed waiting for him and she wondered if she was doing the right thing. Her body was on ten and she couldn't make a rational decision, because she wanted him in her bed, so she decided not to try and figure it out.

Devon looked in on Deja one more time and then he went into the bedroom with Leila. He undressed and climbed under the covers with her. It didn't take long for them to pick up where they had left off.

"You are so beautiful," he whispered and Leila was touched because she hadn't heard that from Devon in years. She relaxed and let him take her body back to places that she never thought she'd go with him again and just when he was about to enter, she stopped him.

"Wait Devon, wait," she whispered. "You need this," she said, reaching over to get the condom she had taken out of the drawer when she got upstairs.

"Are you serious?" he asked her in disbelief.

"As a heart attack," she replied and he knew if he wanted it that was the only way he was going to get it. He didn't want to, but he put it on and made his way into his wife's canal. She released a deep breath and moaned, letting him know that she was happy to have him there. He filled her love nest with divine strokes of his manhood and they felt as one again. She gave herself to him over and over again that night and they made it a point to hit it one more time that morning before they departed.

Leila had no idea where they were going or how they were going to end up. All she knew was that the night before was magical and if their marriage could come back and be that strong, she was willing to try.

XII

Rayshon was ready and he wasn't going to let Leila leave without telling her how he felt or at least asking her out. He was willing to not be her trainer anymore and he had a highly recommended associated he would refer her to if she was willing to go out with him. He was so mad at himself for not saying what he wanted to say to her the other day. He let her leave and didn't say anything because he chickened out and he was not going to back down that day. He had his words down to a science.

Five minutes before her appointment, he was more nervous. He took a shot of scotch to try to calm his nerves, but it didn't help much. He calmed himself as much as he could and sat there watching the clock, waiting for her to knock. Finally, she was there. He walked over to the door and when he opened it, it was Karen. He definitely didn't expect to see her.

"Karen...hey...what are you doing here?" he asked nervously because she caught him off guard.

"Well I was visiting a patient nearby and I thought I'd stop by. I hadn't heard from you and I called you a few times and I really wanted to see you so, here I am."

"Wow, well unfortunately this is a bad time, I got a client…," he tried to say and Leila got off the elevator. She saw him at the door with Karen, but she still approached.

"Hello," she said, speaking to Karen.

"Hi, I'm Karen," she said, being friendly.

"Hi, I'm Leila. Nice to meet you," she said, standing, waiting to go in.

"Hey Leila…, go on in. This will only take a sec," he said, said stepping aside so she could pass. He pulled the door up behind him to address Karen.

"Listen Karen, you are a sweet woman and I had fun hanging out with you, but you cannot drop by my place whenever you feel like it. That is rude to drop by someone's home unannounced."

"Well Ray, I feel that it is rude to tell a woman *'I will call you'* and never call and I also think it is rude to not return a person's phone calls," she said, raising her voice.

"Shhhh," he said, trying to keep his voice down. "Yes you are absolutely right. It was rude and inconsiderate, but you know I conduct my business here. So please don't come here making no scenes and acting out. Now I will talk to you Karen, but please, with all due respect, don't come to my home ever again without calling. I have a client waiting on me and I have to work, so I will call you soon and we can talk, okay?" he said and Karen realized she wasn't dealing with the bullshit ass men she had dealt with previously. Rayshon was a no nonsense guy, so she agreed without dispute.

"Okay Ray, I am sorry."

"No problem," he said calmly and he kissed her hand. She was more taken by him than she was before. She wasn't mad anymore and she walked away with a smile on her face. He stood there for a brief moment and then he walked in. Leila was already upstairs stretching when he went up to join her.

"Hey, thanks for waiting," he said.

"No problem..., I see you were in the middle of something."

"Yeah, but it's all good," he said, ready to get started. He was so happy to see Leila and she was looking radiant, he thought, trying not to stare.

"So, is that your girlfriend?" Leila asked.

"Who?" he asked surprised. He wasn't thinking about Karen anymore.

"Karen," she said, coming up on a sit up.

"No, why would you think that?"

"Because I haven't seen her before and I know how you don't date clients."

"Well my dear, Karen is not my girlfriend."

"Well I will say she is pretty and different from all the others."

"What do you mean, 'different'?"

"Well she seems humble, not territorial. Most of them model looking chicks that I cross in the hall or coming out the door just stare, like I'm a threat to them - especially Christa. I am nowhere near as beautiful as she is, but she always act like you're her man and I'm gon take you. Now, if I looked like her, I wouldn't let any other woman intimidate me."

"She ain't all that," Ray said and Leila paused during the middle of her sit up.

"Come on now Ray, have you not noticed her stomach? No matter how many sit ups you make me do a month, my stomach would never look like that."

"So..., you just had a baby," he said, not liking to hear her putting herself down.

"No, my baby is eight months old Ray and my breasts, even after I'm done nursing, will never be that perky. What man is gonna look at me and want me over a woman like Christa?" she asked and

Ray wanted to say himself, but he didn't.

"Listen Leila," he said, nudging her back down to continue the workout. "Beauty is only skin deep and not all men look at women like Christa and just want them. There are tons of men out there that would want you over Christa," he said, speaking of himself only.

"Yeah, I wish I knew what planet they lived on because I would move there in a New York minute," she said and Ray stood up and walked away.

"What? What's wrong? What did I say?" she asked, wondering what was on his mind.

"Okay," he said and clapped his hands. "Listen Leila, I can't do this anymore."

"Do what? What's going on Ray? Did I do something?" she asked, standing up from the mat.

"No, no, you didn't do anything," he said, moving closer to her. "Look, I tried to deny it and tried so hard to let it go, but I would Leila. I would choose you over Christa any day. You are so beautiful to me and I would do anything if you'd go out with me," he said and held his breath. He had finally told her.

"Ray are you serious? I thought you said that you don't get involved with your clients?"

"I don't Leila and I promise you I've never done anything like this in my life, but I cannot stop thinking about you. You are perfect in my eyes and I wouldn't change one thing about you. You make me laugh and I can't seem to get your pretty smile out of my head," he said and Leila could not believe what she was hearing. She never actually thought of her and Ray ever being anything other than client and trainer, but she knew at that moment why she was jealous of Christa: because all along she thought, he was sleeping with her.

"Me?" she asked in disbelief. She was ordinary and fat. He was finer than Boris Kodjoe and he liked her. It had to be a joke.

"Yes, you," he said and kissed her. It felt so good to finally taste her lips and to hold her close to him. She reached up and put her hand around his neck and they kissed deeply and passionately. They slowed their kiss and he reached for her hands. He kissed her fingers and realized she had her wedding ring back on. She noticed it as soon as he noticed it.

"Look, I didn't expect this Rayshon," she said.

"What's up Leila? Are you and Devon working it out? Are y'all back together?" he asked, disappointed.

"No - well no - I mean, I don't know. I got to be honest with you Ray. I was with him the last couple nights and things felt so right and so good and I was really considering it, but I haven't made that decision yet," she said and he backed up.

"Do you love him Leila?"

"Yes I love him Ray, but it's not the same."

"What do you mean? Either you love him or you don't," he said, feeling like a fool. He wished he had kept his mouth shut and not had shared his feelings with her.

"I love him Ray, but our marriage has been over for a while. You and I have talked about this so many times and you know how I feel. I went and filed my divorce and every since Devon got the divorce papers he has been trying to get back and the last couple nights I was with him, it just reminded me of how things used to be with us. I thought that maybe we had a chance."

"Well that is your answer right there," he said angrily. "Look, I'm sorry for kissing you. I knew it was a mistake in the first place."

"What? Who do you think you are Ray? You tell me five minutes ago that you care about me and you can't stop thinking of me and then you kiss me like you just did and now it was a mistake?" she asked him confused. If he was sure of what he wanted, she could pursue a new avenue.

"Yes, it was a mistake. I opened myself up to a woman who I

thought was done with her past and done with her ex and after I find out that you are still there with him, yes, I made a mistake. I wasn't trying to kiss another's man wife. You told me weeks ago that you filed for the divorce and I understood things to be over and done and it isn't, so kissing you today was a mistake Leila," he said, standing directly in front of her. Although he knew it was not right, he couldn't help but want her.

"It is over Ray. In my heart it is over and my friend asked me the other day was it over and I was too coward to say it. I don't want Devon. I don't love him like that anymore. I was just in love with the idea of us being a family again. I guess I was just caught up in the fact that he was chasing me for a change and I wasn't chasing him. I wanted to be loved and wanted and he was starting to give me what I wanted from him for so long. Even if you and I never be together, I can honestly say it out loud, I don't want Devon. I just want to be loved and treated like a woman," she said, letting the tears fall.

She never gave Devon the final answer because it felt good to be pursued by him. She enjoyed him trying to date her, kiss her and touch her. She liked the fact that he was now begging instead of her. She didn't want him back because he had his chance and when he had her, he treated her horribly. She just was not ready to give up the chase; she wanted to torture him the way he did her when she begged and cried for him to love her.

"Can you allow me to treat you like a woman?" he asked, wiping her tears. He kissed her cheek, then her lips and she let go. Her body started to come alive and she found herself giving in to Ray like a juvenile with no intelligence. She didn't ask any questions, nor did she say a word when he led her downstairs into his bedroom. She had thoughts of Ray before in the past but would always shrub them off because she never thought she'd be a woman that he'd sincerely be interested in. She used to think he was full of shit when he used to compliment her and flirt with her, but as he licked on her body, she thought back to those times and realized he was a grown man not playing any games.

She was glad that she had not sweated a lot and that he

caught her at the top of their workout because he was licking her in places she didn't think he'd give attention to. He was a wonderful lover and she realized what she had been missing for so long. He rubbed her body just right and she was a little embarrassed from the milk from her breasts, but he licked them anyway. She enjoyed his masterful foreplay and took the liberty of helping him put on the condom. She was surprised at herself and how free she felt with him. She wasn't ashamed of her body the way she was with Devon because he didn't hesitate kissing and licking her all over.

When she climaxed, she collapsed on his chest and he flipped her over and finished up the job. He groaned and breathed deeply and she knew he had gotten his too and she laid there smiling because they were both satisfied. She looked over at the clock and their hour session had been over thirty minutes ago. She closed her eyes and drifted off to sleep.

Ray eased up and took a three-minute shower. He came out and left Leila sleeping and he let his afternoon client in. He was on the second floor and he heard Leila's cell phone ring in her purse. He excused himself, ran down and took her purse to her.

"Baby," he said, shaking her a bit, as she opened her eyes. "Your phone was ringing," he said, handing her purse to her.

"Aw, thanks," she said, digging around in her purse and finally retrieved her phone. She looked at her missed calls and it was the store.

"Is everything okay?" he asked her.

"Yeah, just gotta call the store," she said, sitting up.

"Okay, take your time. I gotta get back to my client," he said, standing.

"You still have appointments?" she asked because he didn't kick her out.

"Yeah, 'til six."

"Ray, I can go."

"No, I want you to stay."

"Are you sure?" she asked and he walked back over to her.

"Of course I'm sure. Make your call and I'll be right upstairs," he said and gave her another kiss. She smiled and watched him leave.

XIII

"Renee it's me, Leila," she said.

"Where the hell are you, girl?"

"Guess?"

"You must be with Devon," she said, not very happy about it, but what could she do?

"Nope, I am not with Devon."

"At the salon again?"

"Nope," she said, smiling, pulling the covers over her naked body.

"Well then where?"

"At Ray's," she said, trying to contain herself.

"Okay," she said like 'and?'

"And I am naked in his bed."

"No you are not!" she screamed.

"Yes, I am."

"I thought you said you and Satan, I mean Devon, was getting back together."

"Well girlfriend, I lied."

"You are not moving on Lei. You are shitting me."

"Well Renee, I am moving on and I'm not playing games with Devon. Even if this is nothing between me and Ray, I am living my life for me and I am not gonna let Devon come back when it is convenient for him and turn my world upside down. If he wants to be with Michelle or whomever else, I don't care."

"Well you go girl. I just want you to be sure of what you are doing miss thing, because that Ray, ump, is a sexy mother - shut yo mouth - and you said that a lot of women come in and out of there."

"Well you know what Renee? Life is too short to stress and if he is on some bull you know I will know, so just wish me luck and see how it goes."

"Alright then, so I take it you won't be back to the store today?"

"If you don't mind?"

"Nope, I'm good."

"Thanks, now let me call Devon to see if he can get Deja for me tonight."

"Oh, well good luck with that," she said.

"Tell me about it."

"Well be careful and call me if you need me."

"I will," she said and they hung up. Leila took a deep breath and called Devon and he answered on the second ring.

"Hey baby, what's up?" he said cheerfully and Leila instantly felt like shit.

"Hey Devon, how are you?"

"I am outstanding," he replied as if he was having a good day.

"Hey Devon, listen: can you pick Deja up this evening?"

"Sure not a problem. Where are you going to be?"

"Well I'm gonna go do some shopping. You don't mind, do you?"

"Naw, that's cool. Your place or my place tonight?" he asked as if they were seeing each other again.

"Well I will be by to get the baby tonight," she said nervously.

"Okay then, my place is cool," he said like she would be staying with him and she didn't want to get into with him over the phone, so she agreed.

"Okay then, I'll see you later," she said and hung up quickly. She heard him try to say "I love you," but she ended the call. She put her phone on the nightstand and looked around Ray's room. It was nice and he had good taste, she thought to herself. She got up and wrapped the sheet around her and looked out of the window at the beautiful view. It looked even more beautiful from his bedroom. She stood there and gazed out the window 'til the sound of the music stopped and brought her back. The door was cracked not all the way shut.

She went back over and climbed back into his king-sized bed. It was low to the floor on a mahogany wood platform with matching nightstands. It looked totally opposite of her bedroom, but it was very nice. She looked up over her head at the exposed brick wall behind his bed and admired the décor he had going on in his room. That made her more curious, so she went inside of his bathroom and didn't expect for it to be that massive in size. He had a separated shower and a huge garden tub with jets and had his and her vanities. It was decorated in earth tones with accents of black in the granite and tiled floors.

She went back into the bedroom and could hear voices but couldn't make out exactly what was being said. She relaxed a little 'til she heard, *"You know you want me. I don't see why you keep playing,"* and she recognized that voice it belong to Christa. That trick was literally throwing herself at Ray and Leila felt territorial and she didn't move, until she heard Ray tell her, *"Come on, Christa, it's time for you to go."*

"Ray," she yelled from his room and within moments, he stuck his head in the door. She was nervous and wished she hadn't done that, but when he stuck his head in the door with a big smile on his face, she knew it was okay.

"Yeah," he said, smiling. She could tell he wanted to laugh, but he didn't.

"Can you get me some water, because I'm a little thirsty?" she said with a smirk.

"Um babe, can you come and get it? Because I am with a client," he said and winked.

"I have to come and get it?" she whined.

"Yeah, I am sorta busy," he said, waving her to come out and she got up and wrapped the sheet around her and walked out. He went back over to Christa and her mouth dropped when she saw Leila.

"Oh hi Christa. How was your workout today?" Leila asked and went over to the kitchen and Christa just stood there. Leila grabbed a bottle of water and then she opened the fridge again and grabbed another bottle and walked back into the living area. "Here you go, Christa," she said, handing it to her. "It was nice seeing you again," she said and went back into the bedroom. She stood by the door and listened.

"Oh, so you don't fuck your clients, but you fucking Leila of all people? I could have sworn she was a client, Ray."

"You're right. She was a client and now she's not."

"You know what? I give up, Ray. I don't want your punk ass anyway. I'll see you next week," Christa said and stormed out.

"Well that went well," she heard Ray say before locking the door. She ran and jumped into the bed like she wasn't listening. He walked into the door and jumped on the bed and they burst out

laughing. "I don't want your punk ass anyway," he said, mocking Christa and they continued laughing.

"Oh, so I'm no longer a client?" Leila asked.

"Well I have a guy that I can refer you to. He is good and I know that you will continue to do well" he said and she didn't know to take him seriously or not.

"So, you just gon' dump me just like that?" she asked seriously. She still wanted him to be her trainer. She trusted him and wasn't comfortable with going to another trainer.

"Leila, you know I can't continue to be your trainer if we are together. That is bad for business."

"Ray, you can't just dump me. Need I remind you that we have a contract," she said, sitting up. She wasn't about to let him just push her off to a new trainer.

"Oh yeah, we do have a contract," he said, rubbing his chin.

"Yeah, Mr. Push me off to the side."

"Well how about we just rip up the contract and you work out with me for now on?" he said, smiling.

"Oh, it's like that? You wanna work me out in other ways?" she asked seductively. She felt so comfortable with him and it was like they had been together longer than just that day.

"Yes I would, if you don't mind?"

"I don't mind," she said and they kissed. They were ready to get started 'til a knock came on the door. It was Ray's next client that he just suddenly forgot about.

"Oh baby, I almost forgot my four o'clock," he said, getting up.

"You have another client?" she asked, disappointed that he couldn't stay with her.

"Yes and I have a five and I'll be done," he said, readjusting himself. He was getting excited and it showed.

"Aw, can't you cancel?"

"Hold that thought," he said and made a dash to let his four o'clock in. He went back into the room and got another kiss. He handed her the remote and suggested she watch a little television while she wait. She turned on the tube and flipped through the channels and landed on the HGTV network. She left it there and got comfortable. She dozed off and was in a deep sleep. She felt warm kisses on her arm and it woke her.

"Hey you," he said when she opened her eyes.

"Hey...," she responded, trying to focus her eyes. She had fallen asleep with her contacts in and that was something she rarely did.

"Are you hungry?" he asked.

"Yes, what time is it?" she said, yawning and stretching. Her body felt a bit sore and she knew it wasn't from working out. It was from the sexual encounter.

"Its ten after six," he said, getting up and going into his closet. She reached over, turned on the lamp on the nightstand and looked at her phone. She was relieved that she had no calls from Devon. She sat up and watched Ray pull out clothes from his closet.

"You're done for the day?"

"Yes ma'am and I want you to get up and shower because I am taking you to dinner."

"Okay, I won't argue with you on that," she said, getting up. She was not comfortable with walking around naked in front of him, although she had dropped a few pounds; she was not ready for her close up. "Do you have a robe or something I can put on?" she asked, sitting on the side of the bed, holding the sheet tight.

"Why?" he asked, teasing her. He knew what her body looked like and he was wondering why she was getting shy on him.

"So I can cover up please," she said.

"Why? It's only us. Besides, I wanna watch you walk into the bathroom."

"I'd rather you didn't," she said, turning her head.

"Listen you have to relax, okay? I want you to feel comfortable around me and I want to look at you," he said, coming over sitting next to her on the bed.

"Trust me; you don't wanna look at my body. It's nothing like Christa's or Karen's...," she said and he stopped her.

"Leila, you are Leila and I know that your body is not like Christa's or whomever's. I know that you have stretch marks here," he said, pointing to her stomach, "And I saw your roll right here," he said, reaching around her back, "And I don't have a problem with the way these jiggle," he said, shaking her thighs and it made Leila laugh. "I feel for you and only you. The day I saw you in the bookstore, you were fine and you are fine now, so cut a brother some slack," he said and she felt better, not completely confident, but not as nervous.

"Okay, but if I blind you, don't be trying to sue a sista," she said and got up. She let the sheet drop to the floor and went into the bathroom. She turned on the water in the shower and waited a few moments for it to warm up. Ray came into the bathroom and gave her a fresh towel and looked inside of one of the vanity drawers for a new toothbrush and she saw about ten toothbrushes and she thought he was a player.

"Why do you have so many toothbrushes? Do you have that many women to sleep over?" she asked smartly.

"Ha, ha - the thing is smarty pants, I have clients in and out of here all the time and sometimes after a workout the breath tends to act up, so I have a box in the hall bathroom. I just took a few of them out and put them here for other guests. Trust me, it is just as many left as the day, I put them there. I am not that kind of guy."

"Well Ray forgive me, sometimes I just speak my mind."

"It's cool. I'm not offended."

"Good," she said and stepped into the steamed shower and

she realized the steam was causing havoc to her hair and she knew she'd look crazy after the shower. "You wouldn't happen to have a blow dryer, would you?"

"Now that is something I don't have," he said and she tried to hurry. She didn't want to look a mess, but before she could turn off the water he stepped in with her and she was too excited to deny him what he came for. They caressed each other and made more steam than the hot water. When they were done and finally stepped out of the shower, Leila could have screamed at her reflection in the mirror. She had on no makeup and although her hair was long, the moisture drew it up and the natural curls took form.

She dried her skin and asked Ray to bring her gym bag from upstairs. She had a change of clothes and her hairbrush and makeup bag. She lotion up her skin and then put on her underwear. She brushed her hair back and put it in a ponytail, something she hated to do, but it was the best she could do under the circumstances. She applied a generous amount of eye shadow to enhance her eyes and a nice gloss to make sure she looked presentable for dinner. She came out of the bathroom; Ray was standing in front of his armoire in his boxers and she thought to herself – damn, his back looks good.

She was still wondering if this were a dream. Was this something that was going to go somewhere, or was this just going to be a fling? She stood there and watched him for a moment before she realized she was staring. He turned around and noticed her watching him and she was embarrassed and turned her head.

"What?" he asked.

"Nothing," she said and walked over to her bag on the bed and took out her sweater and jeans.

"Come on Leila, you were thinking something?" he pressed.

"No, I wasn't," she said, lying. He walked over and embraced her from behind.

"Look Leila, I would like for this to go somewhere. I have fantasized about you…about us and I thought this moment would never come and I would like you to always be honest with me, no matter what. I don't care how silly it may be or whatever. If I ask you what you're thinking, it's alright to tell me. If I ask you how you feel, hey, I really wanna know how you feel."

"Okay, I got you. I just can't get over how fine you look and to wanna be with me...I know it is foolish to say, but I'm kinda nervous, you know."

"Well let me tell you this. If at any point I make you feel less than a woman, or if you ever feel anything other than good feelings with me, tell me and I will fix it. I like you Leila, more than I've liked a woman in a long while and I am anxious to see how this will go okay? So relax and trust me."

"Okay, I will try to relax. I've just been with a man who adored me one day and then as soon as one thing changed about me he changed on me and I know that there are beautiful women out there and you come into contact with tons of them. If we're together, I have to be sure that it's me you want."

"Leila, let's just take it one day at a time. Can you do that for me?" he said, touching her face.

"Yes, I can," she said with a bright smile.

XIV

Ray stood at the door of Leila's Armada, freezing for ten minutes because he didn't want to say goodbye. It was already after ten and she had to get to Devon's to pick up Deja. He finally gave her the last kiss and shut her door. He went upstairs feeling like a million bucks. He went to pour himself a shot of scotch and turned on some music. He looked over by the door and realized Leila left her gym bag and he smiled. He was so happy that he told her how he felt and he hoped to get to spend more time with her.

He changed into some sweats and a tee shirt and he couldn't stop smiling. He felt like a young boy in love or with a crush. He thought back to the day when he first saw her at the bookstore and she was sitting behind the counter and acting like she was this married maid and she was off limits. He chuckled when he thought about her say, *"I'll see if my husband would like to come,"* and then after getting to know her and spending time with her she finally shared with him the real deal about her and her failed marriage. From the moment she told him about how Devon left her when she was pregnant, he wanted to protect her.

He started to think of her on the regular from then on. Every session they had, he grew fonder of her. He'd go to the bookstore at least four times a week. Most times, he didn't buy a thing, just pretended to look for something. He started to ask more questions about her personal life, like what was her favorite color and what was her favorite movie and what food did she like more than anything to give him an idea of what she was about. The more they talked, the more he was interested and one day she came for a session and he couldn't help himself. He wanted to touch her. He wanted to kiss her; he realized that he was physically attracted to her.

The day had finally come and he had made his move. He was a bit apprehensive though, because of the conversation they had about her and Devon and how she was considering getting back with him. He knew she was over Devon, or at least he hoped she was over Devon. He tried to relax and not let it get to him. He just decided to take it day by day and see how things go. He was sure that he and Leila would be good together. He was positive that he'd treat her the way she longed to be treated.

He picked up his cell phone and fought the urge to call her. He dialed the number and didn't hit "Talk." He put his hand down to his side and his phone rang in his hand and he looked at the ID. The number looked familiar, but he couldn't remember who it belonged to. He waited a few moments and then he went ahead and answered it.

"Hey, this is Ray," he said.

"Hey, how are you?" the woman's voice said.

"I'm fine," he said, wondering who it was on the other end.

"That's good," she said and he didn't respond. He was trying to recognize the voice.

"Are you still there?" she asked.

"Yeah, yeah, I'm here," he said, thinking to himself, *'who the hell is this?'*

"So, what are you getting into tonight?" she asked.

"Nothing too much…, I just got in from having dinner."

"So, would you like to get into me tonight?"

"Well I don't wanna get into anyone that I don't know. I am trying, but I must be honest: I don't recognize your voice," he said, just finally being honest.

"Well this is Karen," she said and Ray hated he answered the phone.

"Oh, hey Karen. What's going on?"

"Nothing too much, I was just trying to see you tonight. I mean, I know it was foul for me to drop by your place earlier and I do apologize. I just had such a good time with you the other night and I was hoping we can get together and do it again."

"You know I have a tight schedule this week and pretty much during the week I don't do too much because my earliest appointment is normally at five, so honestly I will have to let you know," he said, hoping she'd take the hint and realize that was a brush off.

"Well how about Friday? You know we could get together, see a movie, or get some dinner?" she said, sounding a bit desperate and Ray, normally an honest man, didn't want to just hurt her feelings; he still didn't tell her that he wasn't interested.

"You know what? That sounds good. Let me call you maybe Friday morning to let you know if I can free up some time because I usually take clients at the 24 hour fitness center and right now I may have to get with you later than dinner or movie time."

"Okay, whatever you can work out. Just call me."

"Okay Karen, I will," he said, knowing good and well that he had no intention of doing that.

"Okay, have a good night," she said softly and he felt bad. He knew that Karen was a nice woman and maybe even a good woman, but not the woman he was looking for. He hung up and took his phone over to the charger and plugged it in. He wished he had told Karen the truth and not led her to believe that he'd go out with her on Friday. He wanted to call her back and just tell her the real, but he wasn't in the mood to deal with that situation right then, he was just anxious and ready to talk to Leila. Since she had not called him yet, he figured he'd kill some time by running on the treadmill. She said she would call him once she picked up her baby from Devon's.

He wasn't too happy that she had to go by her ex's house, but he knew that he couldn't do anything about him being her daughter's father. He just wished things were different. He wished that he had met her before she got married, but unfortunately he met her too late. He only hoped that Leila would be strong and not go back.

He got on the treadmill and put on his headset. He ran his normal two miles and decided to do one more. He felt so energetic and hyped; he ran the extra mile without difficulty. He finished and grabbed a towel from the stack of fresh towels that was on the shelf. He wiped his face and stretched. He was so full of energy; he pulled out the mat and did fifty push-ups and one hundred sit-ups. He went over to the mini fridge, grabbed a bottle of water and drank it straight. After a few moments of calming down and getting himself together, he grabbed a few sanitary wipes and wiped everything down.

He went downstairs and hopped into the shower. After he showered and brushed his teeth, he put on a pair of boxers and checked the clock. It was almost one a.m. and he hadn't gotten a call from Leila. He went and checked his cell phone and he had two missed calls, but the number wasn't a number he recognized. He didn't listen to the voicemail from the person that called; he just went and got into bed. He made sure his alarm was set and grabbed his cordless phone to call Leila.

He dialed her cell phone first, it went straight to her voicemail and that made him nervous. He hung up without leaving her a message. He contemplated and contemplated and finally he dialed her house. He waited for three rings before he hung up. He instantly got angry. All he could think of was her in Devon's arms after she left him. How could she look at him and lie to his face? Why did she make him think she was interested in him? Why did she tell him that she was ready to move on if she really wasn't?

He decided that he'd give up. He wasn't in the business of letting women hurt him. Katrina was the last woman that he vowed would hurt him. She was so beautiful and every man wanted her. He met her at the gym and when he first saw her, he thought, *damn, I gotta have that*. He stepped to her and she told him that she had a man and he stepped off. Less than a week later, she was in the parking lot of the gym crying in her car.

When he saw her, he tapped on her window and asked her if she was okay and she said no. Then he asked her if there was something he could do and she said, *"Kill my ex-boyfriend,"* and they started kicking it from there. Everywhere they went; men were always trying to get with her. Even in front of Ray, dudes would step to her. He tried to trust Katrina, but it was hard because she got so much attention.

Every time he'd turn his back, a dude was in her face. He tried to deal with it, but he was so insecure. She assured him that she was in love with him and she didn't want anyone but him, but he couldn't relax. He'd call her every hour on the hour and basically keep tabs on her. He was so worried about her being unfaithful that he couldn't enjoy his relationship. Although she tried to assure him that she was true, he always felt that some dude would be in her ear with some old bullshit and she'd fall for it.

After a year, he finally calmed down. He had no reasons to believe Katrina was untrue because they did everything and went everywhere together. He learned to relax and enjoy his relationship and he stopped stressing Katrina and started acting like a normal boyfriend. He didn't call her fifteen times a day and he didn't ask her twenty questions every time he walked up on her and a guy in her face.

He thanked God for blessing him with a woman that was not only beautiful, but smart and faithful. He eventually fell in love with Katrina and after two years of dating her, he finally proposed. They were engaged, happy and had plans of opening a fitness center together. He was happy and things were going perfect - so he thought.

He worked at the gym full-time and one day a new client saw him talking to Katrina. During their session, his client asked him how did he know Katrina and of course Ray told him that she was his fiancée. When he said that, the guy said, *"Oh, really?"* with a surprised look on his face and Ray asked him, *"What's up, dawg? What's that supposed to mean?"* and the guy just laughed and didn't say anything.

At the end of their session, the client was like, *"Look, dude, I ain't trying to fuck up a happy home, but your girl is foul, believe that."* Ray was like, *"Come on dude, you gotta come with it all, what's up?"* He was like, *"My boy hitting that on a regular, ask your girl about Jay,"* and he walked away. Ray was devastated. He was angry and hurt and he went on a rampage through the gym looking for Katrina; she was nowhere to be found.

He called her back to back on her cell phone and she didn't pick up. Later that evening, after his shift and not being able to reach Katrina, he decided to roll by her spot to talk to her and when he got there, her roommate said she wasn't home and she hadn't seen her. Ray got into his car and went home and when he got there, Katrina was sitting in the hall on the floor waiting for him. When he saw her, he wasn't as angry as he was earlier. He was calm and he didn't go off like he had planned to.

He walked up opened the door and didn't say anything. After a few moments she came inside,

"I was gonna tell you Ray, but I didn't know how," she said softly.

"Tell me what Kat? That you fucking some dude named Jay?" he asked her angrily.

"Baby please, I know that Mike told you today about what he thinks he knows about me and Jay, but I swear that I haven't been with him since you and I got engaged. I swear that we were over a long time ago," she said, lying.

"No Kat, don't play me, tell me the fucking truth. This guy in my face telling me how you are fucking this dude on a regular. Why would he say that if that bullshit has been over?" he yelled. He knew that Mike had to be telling the truth because when Katrina saw that he was Ray's new client, she didn't want to go anywhere near him. She disappeared quickly and if that guy Jay, was a thing of the past why would she have bounced like that? She wouldn't have had anything to worry about.

"Ray please, you know I love you more than anything. I wouldn't lie to you," she said and he didn't believe her. After an hour of arguing and going back and forth, he gave in and gave her the benefit and they made love. He prayed to God and asked him to let Katrina be the woman she said she was and for him to be able to trust her. The next couple of day's things were quiet and good between them like nothing was wrong.

A couple nights after, Ray found out the worst. They were cuddled up in the bed and Ray felt Katrina get up. She went into the front room and she was gone a couple of moments and Ray got up and went into the living room to see what she was doing. He noticed the light coming from the hall bathroom and he eased up close to the door. He stood there and overheard Katrina on the phone talking. It took him a moment, but then he heard her say, *"Jay you have to be patient. I am gonna tell him,"* he didn't want to hear what he heard, but he couldn't walk away from the door. He listened to her conversation on how she was going to break up with him and make her thing with Jay perfect and right.

Ray couldn't believe that he listened to her and allowed her to lie to him and continue to be with her. He was so angry that she lied to him and he let her get away with it. He tried to hold back the tears and not cry, but he was hurt. He went back into his bedroom and laid in the dark and waited for his unfaithful princess to get back into bed. He didn't say anything at first; he just waited for her to snuggle close to him. He laid there for a while and the tears ran down the side of his face in the dark. He moved a little and Katrina readjusted herself and whispered, "I love you Ray," and when she said that he couldn't hold back.

"Get out," he said and Katrina's head popped up.

"What?" she asked in shock.

"Get out...get up and get your lying ass out of my bed," he said and she got defensive.

"Baby what's wrong with you?" she asked him, confused.

"Look, Kat I'm going to say this one time only and I don't want to hear shit from you. I am not a fool, so get up and get your stuff and get out," he said sternly and Katrina jumped up and turned on the lights. She started to gather her things.

"I don't know what's wrong with you, but when you come to your senses call me."

"Trust me Katrina, I won't be calling you."

"Ray, what is wrong? What happened baby, why are you acting so crazy?"

"Kat you gon' act like you just didn't get your trifling ass up and go into my bathroom and call your other man on your cell phone? You actually gon' stand there and look me in my eye and ask me what's wrong with me? What's wrong with you is the question. Now with all due respect and before this gets out of hand up in here, you need to make your exit!" he yelled and she didn't hesitate to get out. She knew Ray and Ray was not the man to be played with.

She left that night and he made it a point to not say another word to her. He didn't ask for his ring back, he just never spoke to her again. She would see him at the gym and he would walk by her as if she were invisible. She tried for months to talk to him, but he simply ignored her and made it a point to not look in her direction. That was one of the reasons he converted his loft into a gym. He got tired of running into to Katrina. He wanted to avoid Katrina at all costs. It had been over five years, almost six since he had been in a relationship after her.

He knew that not all women were the same, but he made it a point to stay away from the drop dead gorgeous women. The women that got extra attention were not the type of women he went after. He was turned off by the women like Christa, Katrina and all the model type *wannabe's* that he trained. None of them did anything for him. Women like that kind were simply trouble and a guaranteed headache. When he met Leila, his heart skipped a beat. She was pretty and average, her beauty was within and that was what he wanted for himself.

He wanted to be with a woman that would be his woman and his only. He wanted a woman that maybe sometimes a man would not glance at twice, not that he wanted an ugly woman, but he wanted an average woman. That was what he thought he saw in Leila, but after that day with her and making love to her he felt otherwise. He felt that she was more beautiful and more attractive than Katrina, Christa and he hoped that he would not have to compete with Devon to have Leila, because he wanted her for himself.

XV

Finally, Leila made it out of Devon's condo. She gave him a million and one reasons why she couldn't stay with him that night. She even lied and told him that he could come over and stay with her the next night so that she could get out of there. She wanted to tell Devon so bad that it was over, but she knew if she did, he would have never let her get out the door. She pulled up at her house at like a quarter 'til one and she knew it was late, but she had to call Ray. She knew she would not be able to fall asleep without hearing his voice.

She hurried inside to get herself situated so she could call him. She put her baby to bed and ran into her room and took off her clothes. Before she could get in her bed and get comfortable to call Ray, her phone rang; it was Devon calling to make sure she and Deja were home safe. She tried to not rush Devon, but he got to talking about their relationship and their marriage and she was about to hang up in his face. Her other line rang and she looked at the ID and saw it was Ray. She tried to make Devon get off, but he kept talking and before she answered Ray had hung up.

"Listen Devon please, I am tired and I have to get up so early in the morning. Please let me call you tomorrow."

"How about I pick you up for lunch tomorrow? We can get a room like we used to do when we first got married and order some room service – and you know…, do what we do," he said.

"Devon come on now, you are moving too fast. Please, you want to do too much," she said with a frown on her face. She was no longer interested in Devon and his antics.

"Okay, okay, you're right. How about just lunch?"

"Lunch is fine, just please Devon, I am exhausted."

"Okay baby, get some sleep. I love you."

"Goodnight," Leila said and hung up quickly. She dialed Ray's number as soon as she heard the dial tone. She got in the bed, pulled the covers up and waited for him to answer. He finally picked up, on the fourth ring.

"Hello," he said in a sleepy voice.

"Hey, are you sleeping?" she asked.

"Yeah, but I'm good," he said, happy that she finally called.

"I'm so sorry I'm calling so late, but Devon is difficult and my battery was dead on my cell phone, so I couldn't call you from the truck."

"No, it's okay. How is your little one?"

"She is fine; in there sleeping her butt off. She is so sweet Ray."

"I can imagine. I can't wait to see her again."

"Really," Leila asked surprised.

"Yes, she is beautiful."

"She gets it from her momma," Leila said, joking.

"She sure does."

"Well listen, I didn't want to keep you up. I just wanted to call you to let you know I was thinking of you and I made it home safely."

"Well you are not keeping me up. I wanna be up and I wish I could be near you."

"Me too...," she said, squeezing her pillow tight.

"So, can I see you tomorrow?"

"Well I don't know Ray. I have to be at my store all day and then I have to get my baby afterwards."

"You can bring your baby along. I just wanna see you Leila."

"Okay, that will be fine if you don't mind if I bring Deja along."

"Why would I mind Leila? I know you are a mother."

"I know, but not too many men wanna be bothered with another man's child."

"Well I'm not your average man."

"You're right about that," she said.

"What do you mean Ms. Leila?"

"Well for starters, you are not the man that I imagined you were when I first met you."

"What type of man did you think I was?"

"Well pardon me, but I thought you'd be an egotistical player. Never in a million years would I have thought you'd be so humble or interested in an average, plus size woman like me."

"Well I am happy that you were wrong about me."

"I am too and I'm still a little afraid, but I'm gonna do what you asked - just take it one day at a time."

"And that is all we can do. I'm still a little apprehensive about you and Devon, but...," he said, being honest.

"Hey, you don't have to worry about me and Devon okay?

That is already a done deal. I just have to finalize my divorce."

"No, you have to get him to sign the papers remember?"

"That's true, but don't worry. Devon will sign them."

"Okay, if you say so."

"Ray please don't worry."

"I'm not worried, but please Leila; in order for me to be happy and continue to be sane I only require your honesty. Don't tell me one thing if there is something else. I will respect you more if you always be honest with me."

"You the same, if you wake up one day and I'm not the one don't make me think that it's all good, just let me know."

"Trust I've been there, so I wouldn't do that."

"With who?" she asked, wanting to know how he's been there.

"That is another story. I'll share it with you one day."

"Okay..., trust that I'll remind you."

"You're a woman, of course you will," he said and they laughed. Ray yawned and Leila knew she had to get off the phone because even though her baby did sleep the entire night, she woke up at six a.m. and she had to get some sleep.

"Listen, I will let you get some sleep, but I will definitely see you tomorrow," she said, reaching over turning on her alarm.

"Call me tomorrow."

"I will. Goodnight," she said.

"Goodnight to you," he said and they hung up. Leila smiled and turned out the lamp on her nightstand. She couldn't remember feeling that excited about a man before. Devon was the first man that she had fallen in love with and she didn't have much experience with men. She had a couple of boyfriends in high school, but nothing big and when she went to college, she met Devon.

They had met at a party and after one dance; he followed her around everywhere she went. She remembers telling her friends that he was stalking her. She couldn't shake Devon back then, so she really was hurt and confused when he turned on her. When he started to treat her cold and started to act like he didn't give a damn about her, it was devastating to her. She cried so many nights for so long and he just would not budge. He would walk out on her when she would get hysterical and leave her by herself to calm down, even when she was pregnant.

She thought back on how she would sometimes call him and he wouldn't answer her calls and how when he was supposed to meet her at a doctor's appointment - and he would not show and when she'd call him and ask him why he'd give her any old excuse and act as if he didn't care. She had her baby's ultrasound pictures hanging on the fridge at her house an entire month before he even noticed and that's when he'd briefly stop by just to so-call 'check on her' or when she'd beg him to come and do chores like mopping or anything that required lifting. He'd come over and help her with the laundry after she'd beg him for days so she didn't have to go up and down the steps.

By the time she was eight months, she needed him to move back home to help her, but he refused and would answer his phone only when he was ready. When she would call him, it would take at least eight or nine phone calls for him to actually pick up. When she went into labor, she had to call Renee because Devon wouldn't answer. Her water broke and of course, she panicked. She didn't know what to do, so she called Devon crying on his voicemail, telling him that she thought she was in labor and to call her back right away. After ten minutes, her contractions started to come and they were strong.

Leila sat on her porch, frantic and unsure if she should drive herself or should she call a cab; she was so nervous and scared she couldn't think. She just called Devon back to back. Finally, she thought of Renee and Renee lived like thirty minutes away. Renee told her to hang tight and she'd be over. Renee made it in twenty minutes and Leila was on the porch, sweating, shaking and crying with her cell phone in her hand. Renee ran inside and got her keys and purse and rushed her to the hospital.

When they admitted Leila, her contractions were three minutes apart. She gave birth in the labor room because there was no time to make it to the delivery room. By the time Devon finally called back, she was in her room with her newborn baby, resting. He got to the hospital and he felt like shit after realizing that he missed his daughter's delivery. He tried to tell Leila that he was in meetings all day and that was the reason he didn't answer and she knew he was lying.

What man in his right mind would not pick up their phone when they know that their wife is in her ninth month, close to her delivery date? Everyone at Devon's company knew that Leila was pregnant and close to delivery and they all knew that their baby was due any day, so Leila knew that he must have been off somewhere doing some other business. Plus, she called his office and his assistant said he wasn't in, so she just looked at him and didn't say a word.

When he picked Deja up out of the little bassinet, he sat down, broke down and cried. He made all of them fake promises to Leila, promising her that he wouldn't leave her side, that he was going to get his act together and come home and be a father to Deja and a husband to her. He vowed that he would be a better man and that lasted for about the first month of Deja's life. He had moved back home for about six weeks.

After her six-week check up, when she was able to move around and handle Deja better, Devon went back into Devon mode. He went back to not coming when he said he would and not answering his phone when he didn't want to answer his phone. Leila went back to crying and moaning and Devon went back to not caring. They'd have a good week or a good few days and then back to a horrible week and a horrible few days. Leila would plead and beg and Devon would lie and make empty promises.

She gave him chance after chance because she just couldn't get over him. She allowed him to spend the night when he wanted to spend the night and she gave him her body whenever he wanted her.

She always had hopes that her husband would come home and be with her. Then he finally told her that he wanted a divorce. He said he would file for a divorce time after time, but he never presented her with papers. He would tell her on Monday that he didn't see a chance for them to get back together and then on Thursday he would tell her he loved her and he was sorry for putting her through hell.

Now Leila was strong and ready to re-establish her life. She finally had sense enough to shut Devon down and all of a sudden, his intentions were finally genuine. He was home more, answered his phone each and every time Leila called and wouldn't hesitate to be right there for her when she needed him. She hadn't seen or heard about Michelle and Devon was really showing heartfelt interest in getting back with her.

He said over and over that he didn't want the divorce and Leila was starting to believe him. Although she knew that she was at the point where she couldn't trust Devon and she really didn't want him back. She was just caught up in the idea of them getting back together. She felt that for the sake of the baby that if he wanted to come back she should let him, but deep down that wasn't what she sincerely desired. She loved Devon - yes, but the romantic love for him was gone. She was no longer taken by his presence in a room.

She no longer missed him when he wasn't around. She no longer cared if he called or stopped by. She was at the point in her life where living without him was something she could live with, but before it was not like that. She was relieved that she could go day to day without crying. She had finally had peace with him no longer being in her life. She went out and did it. She filed for divorce so she could be free to be happy and *'now he wanna come back.'*

XVI

Ray got up at four thirty with no problem. He showered and brushed his teeth while he bobbed his head to the music that filled his loft. He knew his neighbors were cursing him out for listening to music that early and so loud but he didn't care. He was ready to face another day because he was anxious to see Leila again. His first appointment was there on time and he got started right away. The session went by quickly and before he knew, it was five o'clock and he was opening the door for his last appointment, or so he thought.

When he opened the door, it was Katrina and Ray had to blink twice. He stood there staring at her. He could not believe his eyes. He didn't say anything; he just looked at her.

"Hi Ray can I come in?" she asked.

"What do you want?" he asked, looking at her like *'how dare you ask me can you come into my house when you disrespected my house by calling your man?'*

"I need to talk to you. I need talk to somebody," she said and started crying. "I have nowhere else to go Ray, please," she said, sobbing and he let her in. He closed the door and let her have a seat.

He glanced at the clock and knew that Mia would be there in a couple seconds.

"Look Kat, I am sorry, but I have to work. My five o'clock will be here any minute."

"Please can I just hang out here for a while? I promise I won't get in the way. I just..., I..., I ...," she tried to talk, but she was upset. The door had a knock and Ray knew it was Mia.

"Listen, you can wait here, but understand whatever it is I can't help you," he said and opened the door. Mia came in and saw Katrina sitting on the couch crying, so she paused.

"Do we need to reschedule?" she asked Ray.

"No, come on in. Just go on up and I'll be up in a sec," he told Mia. She went up and he turned his attention to Katrina. She looked bad, not the way he remembered her and he wasn't sure what her dilemma was, but he was definitely sure he didn't want to get involved. "Look Kat, I will be an hour, so sit tight. If you're hungry or need something to drink help yourself."

"Okay...," she said softly and nodded her head up and down. He turned to go up stairs and she called his name and he turned to look at her.

"Yes...?" he said.

"Thank you...," she said, looking sad.

"Don't worry," he said and went on up. It seemed like the session with Mia was forever. When it was finally over, he went down to let her out and Katrina was sleeping on the sofa. He let Mia out and didn't wake Katrina. He sat there and looked at her and realized she had stains on her clothes and they looked oversized, like they were not hers. He looked at her handbag and it looked like it had some clothing items in it and he wondered what in the hell was going on with her.

She was sleeping so hard, he didn't want to wake her because she looked like she needed rest. He stood up and went back upstairs to wipe down everything, like he normally did after every session. He went back down and went into the kitchen and he saw that Katrina helped herself to a sandwich because she left all the fixings on the counter. He cleared away everything and went back to check on her and she was dead asleep. He took a deep breath and asked himself why he let her in. He went over to his cell phone and called Leila because he knew that it wasn't a good idea for Leila and Deja to come over 'til he figured out what was going on with Katrina.

"Hey Leila," he said when she answered.

"Hey you. What's going on?" she said, delighted to hear his voice.

"Listen, something has come up and I may have to see you tomorrow," he said and that immediately disappointed Leila. She had been waiting anxiously all day to see him and now he was calling to say that he could not see her.

"Why, what's going on?" she asked and he could hear the disappointment in her voice.

"I'm sorry, but a friend of mine is in trouble and I have to help my friend out?"

"Oh okay, I'm sorry. Is there anything I can do?"

"No, but thanks and I promise I will call you a little later."

"Okay, I will be at home."

"Okay babe. Take care and I will call you back soon."

"Okay, just take care of your friend."

"Thanks for understanding," he said and they hung up. He went to shower and change. When he came back, Katrina was still sleeping. He didn't bother her; he just let her sleep. It was close to ten when she finally opened her eyes. He was sitting in the chair watching television with the volume low when she sat up. He looked over at her and she had a look of surprise on her face.

"Did you sleep well?" he asked and she stretched.

"Yes, what time is it?" she asked.

"It's a quarter 'til ten," he said.

"Oh, it's that late? You let me sleep Ray?" she asked, surprised.

"Yes I did. You looked like you needed some rest."

"Yes. I am very tired."

"Are you hungry?"

"Yes, I am starving," she said and stood. "Can I use the bathroom?"

"You know where it is," he said and got up to go into the kitchen to heat her up some chicken, rice and steamed vegetables. He set the plate of food on the table along with a bottle of water and waited 'til she came out of the bathroom. She sat back on the sofa, he pointed at plate and bottle of water for her and she opened it and took a swallow.

"Kat what's the deal? Why are you here?" he asked when she finally put the empty plate on the coffee table.

"Well I tried calling you twice last night and I left you a message, but you didn't call me back. I figured you wouldn't, so I came to talk to you face to face."

"About what? What do you wanna talk to me about?"

"Listen Ray, I know I'm the last person you want to see right now, but I am in a jam. I need a place to crash 'til I can save up some money to get me a place. I have been living in my car for the last couple days and I don't have any place to go."

"What about your mom's? Go to your mom's," he suggested. He knew Katrina's mom and he knew no way she would have Katrina living in her car.

"Ray my mom is dead," she said and the tears rolled down her face.

"What? When? What happened?" he asked. He knew Katrina's mom well and he had no idea she passed.

"About three months ago. She had gotten really sick a year ago and I moved her in with me to take care of her. When she was living with us, things got worse for her and it caused problems with me and…," she hesitated, then continued. "Jay just wasn't happy to help me with my sick mother and we argued and argued and when my momma died I was depressed and he wasn't there for me and it was like he didn't care. Anyway, things didn't get any better and about a month ago, he put me out. I stayed at Yvonne's, but I messed that up too and she threw me out. She wouldn't let me come in and get my things because it was some shit about me supposedly sleeping with her man and I didn't, I swear, he just wanted me and she knew he was after me, so I have been just down and out. When momma died, she had no insurance, so I wiped out my savings burying her and I am broke.

"I'm gon' lose my job if I don't get it together. I was in a motel for a couple of days, but I have no money Ray. My car note is due. I am behind in everything and my life is so out of control. I just need somebody to help me," she said, sobbing out of control. Ray got up and went to get her a tissue and he sat down beside her and held her. He felt bad for her, but he was in no position to help her. Not the way she wanted him to, because she definitely couldn't stay there.

"Listen Katrina, I am sorry about your mom and I will help you, but you cannot stay here. I am involved with someone and I don't want any drama and confusion around here. I will get you a room and try to pay on some things for you, but you have to stay away from here. We are not friends anymore, but I can't leave you out there. I will get you a room for a couple weeks and get things straight with your car so you don't lose your transportation, but that's it. That is all I can do for you."

"That's fine Ray, anything will help me at this point and I promise I will pay you back every dime when I get on my feet," she said, looking him in the eyes. He had to turn away from her because the emotions and feelings he had for her at one point were trying to creep up.

"Look Kat, you don't have to pay me back," he said, getting up going over to his desk to get his checkbook. He asked her how much did she owe on her car note and she got up and sat near him at the desk. He wrote the check out for the balance she had to pay and it was for two payments. He wrote the check to her finance agent and handed it to her. He told her that he knew a guy that ran a hotel that he used to train and he was sure he could get her in for a few days and he made a phone call. He told her that he'd give him one month and he gave Ray a first-rate discount. He gave him Katrina's information for her to check in without him.

"Listen, the hotel is nice and they serve breakfast every morning. Here is some cash to get you going," he said, giving her a couple hundred dollars. He had done way more than enough. Fifteen hundred dollars for her, to be exact and if that wasn't enough, oh well he thought and he tried to hurry to get her out of his hair. It was almost eleven and he wanted to see Leila.

"Thank you again," Katrina said to him for the hundredth time. He didn't want to hear thank you another time, he just wanted her gone. "I promise...," she tried to say.

"Listen Kat, don't worry about it. I just want you to take care of yourself and I wish you the best of luck," he said, holding the door, waiting to close it.

"Thanks Ray, you are a lifesaver."

"Take care Kat," he said and shut the door. He couldn't stay in her presence any longer. He straightened up the couch and pillows and went into the kitchen to pour out the unfinished water she left behind. He searched for his cell phone and quickly dialed Leila's number and he was happy when she answered on the second ring.

"Hey Leila, are you up?"

"Yes, how are you?"

"Better now to hear your voice," he said.

"Me too, but I am gonna have to give you a call back, if that's okay. I am in the middle of something right now," she said and his heart went south.

"Devon…," he said, disappointed.

"Yes…," she said and he knew that he may not hear from her anymore that night.

"Okay, call me back no matter how late."

"Oh I will, trust me," she said and he felt a little better. It was obvious she was thinking about him too.

"Okay bye," he said and hung up. He went into the kitchen and poured himself a drink. He didn't know what to think or what to do. Was Devon there putting the moves on Leila or was she laying down the laws? He was mad at himself for letting Katrina stay and sleep so long at his place because he missed out on seeing Leila. He should have woke her up right after Mia left and let her share her sob story and got her out the damn door, but no, he allowed her to ruin his evening and he was pissed. He sat on the sofa and grabbed the remote. He looked at the clock and hoped that Leila would call him back soon

XVII

Leila sat there wondering why Devon did not understand where she was coming from. They went over the same thing five times and he still didn't accept the fact that she wanted a divorce from him.

"Devon I tried. I really tried to consider everything you've said and I am not saying that there is no love left in my heart for you because that would be a lie. I just know that there was too much damage done and I don't want to go back to what we had because eighty percent of that time I was miserable."

"I know Lei and I know that I made bad choices and I know that I've made horrible mistakes. I wish that I could take it all back honey. I really wish that I could, but I can't. I just want to make it right now. I want to make it up to you. I was an idiot Lei, please don't leave now. I know we have what it takes to make it. You just have to try."

"That's the thing Devon, I don't wanna try. I don't wanna try anymore. I've tried for more than two years to make it right and all you did was toy with me and made threats and criticize me. I allowed you to dictate my days by doing things according to you. Trying to not say the wrong thing, to keep you from walking out on me. I bent over backwards trying to please you."

"And I am willing to bend over backwards to please you Leila," he said, getting up and moving closer to her. He took her hands and held them tight. "I want to do whatever it takes to make this work."

"Devon," she said, looking him in the eyes. "I don't want to hurt you. I don't want to break your heart baby, because I know how that feels, but I am sorry. What we had is gone. I don't love you the way I did before and I have grown accustomed to being without you and I don't see where I fit in your lifestyle. You and I are not the same and I don't want to point fingers Devon, but it is because of you, that I am who I am today. I loved you so desperately at one point and I don't feel like that anymore. Now please, if you want me to be happy, don't fight me. You know you don't want this Devon."

"I do, I swear I do Lei," he said with tears in his eyes. Her heart was aching because he seemed so earnest and ready, but that opportunity was gone and she didn't want him anymore.

"I know you do baby," she said and hugged him tight. She sat there with him for a few moments and they held hands. She didn't say anything else because there was nothing left to say. She had made her decision and her heart ached for Devon, because he was now the man she had married - the man that she remembered falling in love with. The man she had hoped so many nights would return to her.

"Devon please understand that I don't hate you and it is killing me to see you hurt, but don't fight me on this. I will always be here for you and you will always be in my heart."

"Don't say that Lei. I'm begging you; I don't want this."

"Devon, I'm so sorry," she said, sticking to her guns. She couldn't back down. She couldn't let him persuade her to give in to him.

"I won't sign those papers. I know that we are meant to be; it's just gonna take time for you to realize," he said and stood. He grabbed his keys to leave.

"Devon don't do that baby. Don't fight me. Please don't drag this out. Give me the divorce so we both can move on with our lives."

"But I don't want to move on. I want you."

"Why Devon? Why now?" she yelled.

"Because I love you Lei. Why is that so hard for you to believe?"

"Because you've treated me like a man that didn't love me for the past two and a half years. You walked out, that's why Devon. You left me when I was pregnant Devon. I had to deal with your lies, your empty promises. You criticized me about my weight and called me names, hurtful names and then to add to my sorrow, when I needed you the most, you packed your things and moved out."

"I never stopped loving you."

"What…, you thought you could take a marriage vacation and then come back into your marriage when it was convenient for you and expect things to be the same?"

"No, I just never thought a day would come that you didn't love me anymore."

"I never thought a day like this would come either Devon, but it has and I just want a divorce. I want to be free to start over and try new things and be happy."

"You can start over and I know I can make you happy Lei."

"I'm sure you can Devon, but that isn't what I want anymore, we are not an option anymore."

"So, it's really over?"

"I'm afraid so," she said and Devon's heart was in horrible agony. He didn't know why he wanted to make things work with Leila now, but he did. He was tired of playing bachelor and he wanted to make a new start and leave the single man's life alone. He looked at Leila for a few moments and he walked away. He got to the door and paused before leaving.

"Leila I won't fight you, but I will pray that you reconsider your decision and before this is final I hope that we both end up with what we both want."

"Me too Devon...," she said.

"I love you Lei, don't ever forget that."

"I know Devon and I loved you once too. I'm sorry things had to come to this."

"Yeah, I know. I'll see you tomorrow, when you pick up the baby."

"Okay drive safe," she said and he finally left. She was glad that she had gotten that over with. She looked at the clock and it was after twelve, but it didn't matter; she wanted to call Ray. She turned off everything and set her alarm and went upstairs. She stopped in to check on her baby and to her surprise, Deja was up.

"Hey baby girl, what are you doing up?" she asked her baby as she picked her up out of her crib. Her diaper was wet. "Oh, you are soaked. I see why you are up," she said and changed her diaper. She took her into her room with her and propped her up on a pillow and turned on the television. She put on the movie Shrek 3 and turned the volume up a little. It was one of her favorite movies and she always put it on for Deja.

A few months ago, Deja would watch and say nothing, but she was now making sounds and smiling at the television. She got into bed and grabbed her phone and dialed Ray's number. He answered on the third ring and she knew she woke him up.

"Hey you," he said when he picked up.

"Hey," she said, smiling and he could hear the smile in her voice.

"I thought I wouldn't hear from you 'til tomorrow."

"Why? I told you I'd call you when I was done."

"How'd it go?"

"Okay, I guess. I'll just have to see how it goes. Devon was pretty upset, but I think that he understands that there is nothing left."

"Are you positive that's what you want?"

"Yes, for the hundredth time, I'm sure."

"Okay, if you say so."

"Yes, I'm saying so."

"So, how is your daughter?" he asked, sitting up in the bed. He was no longer sleepy.

"She is fine; sitting up here wide awake."

"No way, it's after midnight."

"I know right, but she's right here with her momma, keeping me company."

"I wish I was keeping you company."

"What's stopping you?"

"I don't know, you tell me?"

"Well for one, it's late and two, its cold outside."

"Well I guess that means we have to wait another night?"

"Yeah I guess, unless you wanna come over here?"

"Are you serious?" he asked.

"Yeah I mean, I don't mind you coming over and I do wanna see you," she said, smiling. She knew it was a bit risky asking him to come over, but Devon didn't live there anymore and he allowed Michelle to come over to his place.

"You know what time it is, right?"

"Yes, do you have a curfew?"

"No, but I have a five a.m. client."

"Oh I'm sorry. I forgot you start early."

"Yes, that is the down side. I normally would be knocked out at this time. I get to stay up late on Saturday nights because no appointments on Sundays.

"So, I guess tomorrow?" she said.

"Sadly, but yes," he replied.

"So, what time will you be done tomorrow?"

"Well I had a cancellation at 1:00. Do you think you could break free?"

"Well Renee and Nicki are both there on Saturday's, so I can sneak away for a little while."

"Cool," he said.

"So, tomorrow at one right?"

"Yes ma'am."

"Well I'll be sure to be there."

"I'm happy to hear that."

"So, I'll see you tomorrow then?"

"Yes, tomorrow," he said and yawned again.

"Okay, I will let you go so you can get some sleep and be well rested for me tomorrow."

"Oh trust, I'll be rested," he said and couldn't help yawning.

"I gotcha. Goodnight," she said and they got off the phone. She didn't have to get up as early as he did and she had to figure out how she was going to get her baby to sleep. "Okay, come on DJ, it's time for you to go to bed baby," she said, taking her into her nursery.

"Dah, dah, dah, dah," Deja said, reaching over Leila's shoulder as if she were looking for Devon.

"Daddy isn't here sweet pea," she said, trying to put her down in her crib and she began to kick and scream and Leila was surprised to see her behave that way.

"Dah, dah, dah, dah," Deja cried, reaching her hands and kicking her little chunky legs.

"Deja, what's wrong, baby? Your daddy isn't here," she said, picking her up and she cried for Devon as she rubbed her little sleepy eyes. That made Leila want to call Devon to come back over, but she quickly decided against it.

"Hell naw, I'm not calling him and you are going have to cut it out sweet pea and go your little behind to sleep," she said and put Deja in the bed with her. After she fussed for a little while, she stopped crying and went on to sleep. Leila took her back to her crib and realized that Deja knew who Devon was. She thought it may be a bad idea to take her around Ray since Deja could distinguish who her daddy was. She didn't want to confuse her with another man.

She climbed into bed and smiled because she was going to see him and get some more of his good loving and that made her shake. It was so good and she knew he had what it took to make her weak. Her last thoughts were his back when he was standing in front of his armoire and she drifted off to sleep.

XVIII

"Okay, I'll see you next week," Ray said to his client as he opened the door and Leila was standing outside getting ready to knock. When he saw her, his man jumped in his pants. He was delighted to see her and couldn't wait 'til she arrived that afternoon. He had been counting the minutes, anticipating the moment that he could kiss her lips again. As soon as he shut the door, he grabbed her and kissed her and then gave her a soft kiss on the forehead.

"Hello to you, too," she said.

"Hey," he said and returned a smile.

"I see someone is happy to see me."

"Oh I can't tell you how anxious I was and I don't wanna waste too much time standing out here talking," he said, pulling her closer to him and they kissed again. They broke long enough for her to follow him into his bedroom. He started undressing her, making sure he kissed her neck and her shoulders. He turned her away from him and kissed her back and Leila closed her eyes and allowed his hot breath to caress her skin. He made a point not to miss a spot as he kissed her down her back and slid her panties down. He kissed her on the back of her thigh and she let out a deep breath.

Her knees began to go weak and her spot began to moisten

because he was turning her on. He wrapped his arms around her waist and kissed her ass cheeks and then he slowly moved back up to her back and then her neck. Leila moaned and the sound of her heavy breathing let him know that he was on the right track. He sucked on the side of her neck and massaged her breasts from behind. She closed her eyes and enjoyed the warm kisses that he planted on her skin and wished that her breasts were empty because the more he massaged them the more she wanted him to suck them.

He massaged them so good that she began to leak milk and she was totally embarrassed. "I'm sorry," she said after they both realized the milk was running down his forearm. He turned her to face him and kissed her lips and said, "You don't have to apologize Leila, this is a natural thing.

"I know, but it is so not sexy," she said and they laughed.

"Yeah, it is a little different from what I'm used to, but I'm okay," he said and went into the bathroom to get a towel. He wiped his forearm and hand and handed the towel to Leila and she wiped her stomach.

"Thanks," she said after dabbing her nipples and handing him the towel.

"Look, this is not a big deal. I'll just have to be gentle," he said and kissed her left breast softly. "And I will try to resist the urge to suck on them."

"You think you can resist? Because I wish you could suck on them."

"I know, but these belong to Deja right now, so that means I won't get to pleasure these the way I wanna, 'til a little later on down the line," he said, like they had a future together and that made Leila smile.

"Later on down the line, huh?"

"Yeah, if you allow me to be around you for a while," he said nibbling on her neck and she let out a deep breath.

"How do you know that you will want to be around me for a while?" she asked as he softly kissed her neck.

"Well so far I feel like this is gonna go far, but you and I just will have to see won't we?" he said, pulling her closer and squeezing her tighter. They moved over to his bed and she laid back and he kissed and licked her nipples as softly as he could, trying not to disturb the milk, but they still leaked a little. She closed her eyes and let him lick her everywhere. She had thoughts of the way Devon used to make love to her and how he used to do her body just as good as Ray was doing her, 'til she put on the weight. She remembered how he used to make her body scream, but after the pounds, all she got was a good pounding with her shirt or nightgown on covering her body.

She was grateful for that, due to the lack of sex she was getting, so the charity sex Devon had been giving her back then didn't have nothing on the way Ray was putting it on her. He was giving her buckets of pleasure and she didn't want him to stop, even if a fire broke out.

"Aw baby, please don't do that," she moaned.

"You want me to stop?" he asked and he knew she did not. He was licking her spot and she hadn't had oral in so long her clit was already ready to climax after a couple moments of him licking her.

"No, I don't want you to stop," she said between deep breaths and pants. "Oh baby..., oooh, that's good, aw..., .aw..., baby, that feels so good," she said and then she orgasm after only two or three minutes.

"Damn..., you came?"

"Yes, yes and I can't believe it," she said, embarrassed at the way her body jerked.

"Wow, that is a new record for me," he said and kissed her inner thigh.

"It's been so long since I've had that done to me and your

tongue is like magic," she said and he smiled.

"Oh so you liked that?" he asked climbing on top of her.

"Oh yes, I did like that baby," she said and they kissed. She rubbed his back and they rolled over. She kissed his chest and rubbed his erection through his shorts. She wanted to do to him what he had just finished doing to her, so she pulled away his shorts and boxers. He relaxed and allowed her to take his man inside of her mouth. The warmth and wetness of her mouth was so pleasing to him that he groaned with excitement. He was impressed with Leila's performance and knew he was working with a woman who knew what she was doing and that made him more excited. After only a few moments of her professional work, he was ready to burst.

"Aw Leila, baby yes…, yes baby…, yeah," he moaned. He rubbed the back of her head and concentrated really hard so he wouldn't explode in her mouth. "Oh yeah, ooh shit…, baby," he said and he was close to losing it. He hadn't had good head in a long time and Leila was giving her superstar performance. "Ah baby, stop…, no baby stop…, I'm gon' bust…, please," he said, trying to pull her off. He couldn't hold onto it any longer. She eased up and did what he asked her to do.

"Damn girl, you get down like that?" he asked and she smiled. She was happy to know that she pleased him just as much as he pleased her.

"You like that?" she asked, rubbing her fingertips over his erection.

"Come here," he said, grabbing her face. He kissed her passionately as he forced his weight onto her. He reached over in the nightstand drawer and got a condom and quickly ripped it open and put it on. She laid there looking at his beautiful chest and washboard stomach and still could not believe she was in bed with him. Even as he rolled the condom on, she thought she had to be dreaming. Devon was good looking - yes, slim - yes, but his body was nothing like Rayshon Johnson's body.

He leaned in and kissed her again before he pushed himself

inside of her. After a few pumps, he pushed Leila's legs back further, making sure he got as deep as he could. Her tunnel was soaking wet and he could hear her juices pop as he stroked her. "Aw, aw, aw," she moaned as he gave himself to her. It was even better to him than it was the first time they had done it.

"Oh baby, your pussy feels so good," he said with his eyes shut. He was enjoying every stroke and she was too. "Leila baby…, aw baby," he continued to moan. He rested on top of her and put his tongue in her mouth as he rolled around in her love nest. It was so good he sucked her chin and licked her neck. He wanted to eat her up at that moment. They were sweating and moaning and used their entire hour going at it. He was in mid-stroke from behind her on their second round and his next appointment knocked at the door.

"Damn, what time is it?" he asked, still pumping.

"Baby, I think I heard the door," she said, not answering his question. She was on her knees facing the window and she couldn't see the clock.

"I know, but its right there baby," he said, still pumping and his client knocked again. He pumped faster and he came. "Oh, oh, oh damn…, aw…, aw…, aw," he said, trying to keep from collapsing onto Leila. They were sweaty and the aroma in the air from their lovemaking indicated he needed a shower before going near his client.

"Baby, the door," she said again and he pulled out.

"I know baby, I know," he said and went into the bathroom. He came back with a robe. "Here, put this on and tell Nina to give me ten minutes," he said and Leila looked at him strange.

"You want me to go out there looking like this?" she asked, surprised.

"Come on babe, I gotta shower," he said and she got up and put on the robe to do exactly what her man asked her to do. "Thanks," he said and ran to get into the shower. By the time Leila made it to the door, Nina was halfway down the hall, but she heard the door, so she stopped and went back up.

"Nina," Leila said, making sure it was her.

"Yes," she replied, confused to see Leila in a robe.

"Come on in. I'm Leila," she said, introducing herself with a smile.

"Leila," she said, looking around wondering what was going on. Leila was in a robe with her hair mangled and she knew Ray's rule about messing around with clients.

"Listen, Ray asked me to tell you to go on up and stretch and he'll be with you shortly," she told Nina and from the look on Nina's face Leila could see she was not happy to see her in a robe and looking like she had just gotten done screwing.

"Where is Ray?" she asked with attitude.

"Well he's in the shower," Leila said, pointing to his bedroom.

"Oh really?" Nina said and headed for the steps. "Tell him not to keep me waiting long. I am a paying customer," she said and rolled her eyes. Leila just laughed it off and headed back into the bedroom. Five minutes later Ray came out and began to dry his skin.

"How'd it go? Is Nina upstairs?"

"Oh yeah, she is up there alright," Leila said and got back into Ray's bed.

"What does that mean?"

"She told me to tell you to hurry up because she is a paying customer; like I'm not."

"She didn't mean it like that," he said, stepping into his boxers.

"Yeah, whatever."

"Baby, don't pay them any attention okay?" he said, wishing Leila wouldn't let his female clients get to her.

"Yeah, easy for you to say. Christa looks at me like I'm shit and Nina just looked at me like I am a fat monster. I wonder what the rest of them will think after they all know that you and I are seeing each other. When the all find out that Ray chose the fat girl," she whined.

"Baby you are not fat and I don't care what they think okay and neither should you. Now, how long do you have because I got to head upstairs?" he asked, pulling his tank top over his head.

"I'm good. I'll hang out here for a while."

"Okay…, you can shower if you want. Towels are in the linen closet. Help yourself to the fridge and make yourself at home. Eventually they will all know and I'm happy with the choice I made, so fuck'em," he said and leaned in to kiss her. "Be done soon."

"Okay babe, I'm cool. Go on," she said with a weak smile. She wondered why women acted so evil toward one another. Why was she getting the dirty looks and the frowns? She was just as beautiful as the next woman was and her size twelve body was alright for her and Ray, so she didn't understand.

She got up and went into the front and got the bag she brought with her so she could shower. She remembered to put her blow dryer and curling irons in that time, to make sure she could look better than she did the last time she was there. She showered and dried her hair and put a few curls in her hair. She put on a little make up and she knew the glow she was wearing was from her afternoon lovemaking with Ray. She went into kitchen to grab a bottle of water and she overheard Nina and Ray upstairs talking.

"So, are you fucking her Ray?" she heard Nina ask.

"Excuse me, where do you get off asking me about my personal business?" Ray asked her.

"Christa was right?"

"So, Christa going around telling my business?"

"Well Ray, we are just all wondering how we have flirted and tried to hook up with you and as soon as big momma start coming you decide to just hook up with her? Now, I understand you not wanting to hook up with Christa and some of them other hoes, but over me Ray? What's up with you?" she asked and Leila was shocked to hear her acting so childish and bold.

"Nina, your session is over and you need to keep your opinions about Leila and my other clients to yourself and not forget that we have a business relationship and I don't have to explain to you why or who I choose to see or date. You and your little chatty friends are starting to wear me out. Now, if you would like to keep coming and continue doing business with me, I'd advise you to keep your nose out of my personal affairs."

"Okay Ray damn, I gotcha. Just tell me this: what does she have that I don't?" she asked, moving closer to him and he stepped back a little.

"Nina my darling you are a beautiful woman and any man that can see would not look past you, but to keep our relationship professional, my answer to that question is simply nothing," he said and the expression on her face let him know that that answer wasn't the answer she was looking for.

"Nothing?" she asked confused, with her hand on her hip.

"Ok," he said, scratching his head. Nina was gorgeous - yes, but she wasn't too bright. "Listen, that means that I am attracted to women. I am just as attracted to Leila as I would be to you. She is just as beautiful, funny and sweet as you are in my opinion," he said, hoping she got it that time, but the way she stood there with the simple look on her face made him know it was useless. "Listen Nina, I gotta get ready for my next client. Will I see you for your next session?" he asked, making sure she wasn't too pissed off.

"Of course…, I'll be back. I can't just hand my body over to another trainer," she said and winked. She turned to leave and rolled her eyes as she headed down the steps. Leila was sitting on the sofa drinking her water when she came down.

"Leila," she said and Leila wanted to cuss.

"Nina," she returned and got up to follow her to the door. Nina was disappointed that she was not the one Ray chose, but she was cool.

"Look Leila, my apologies for earlier and you my sista are lucky because this one is definitely not an easy win," she commented, pointing at the ceiling because Ray was still upstairs.

"I've heard," Leila said, although she disagreed because she didn't have to chase or play games or throw herself at him to get him.

"Yeah and trust he's a good guy, so good luck to ya' because I know at least sixty percent of his female clients are gonna be pissed and they are not a nice crowd," she said, trying to give Leila the heads up.

"Thanks Nina. That's good to know," she said, returning a warm smile.

"Okay then Leila, it was nice to meet you and I guess I'll be seeing you around."

"Nice to have met you, too," Leila said, holding the door open for Nina to leave. She shut it behind her and felt a little better to know that Nina was at least human and not all bitch.

"Hey," Ray said, coming up behind her.

"Hey," she said and he pulled her close and kissed her.

"Listen, I'm sorry about that. You know I have a lot of female clients and a lot of them have tried to hook up, so it is going to be a lot of upset women for the next few weeks 'til they all get used to you."

"I see," she said, putting her head down.

"Leila baby, please don't let them get to you. I'm with you because I wanna be okay, so just ignore their asses. Fuck their attitudes, snide remarks and negativity," he said, lifting her head.

"Well Ray, are you sure I'm what you want because I am not worried about them and I'm a grown ass woman and I could care less about what them bitches think or say about me or if they think I'm a big momma," she said and he didn't know that she overheard Nina. "I just wanna make sure you are okay with it?"

"I'm perfectly fine," he said and smiled. She smiled back and was about to kiss him, but there was a knock at the door. "That's Samara," he said, getting her ready for the next bitch that he provided his services to.

"Should I get that?" she asked.

"Yeah you should and make sure you introduce yourself," he said and headed for the steps. She turned and took a deep breath and opened the door to another drop-dead gorgeous woman and she just shook her head and told herself, *'this is only the beginning.'*

XIX

"Come on Devon, I need to go. You said you'd watch DJ this weekend, now you backing out at the last minute," she asked, pissed at him.

"No Lei, I'm not backing out. I'm asking you where you are going."

"And I'm telling you again, none of your business," she said, irritated.

"Well if you can't tell me where you're going, I can't keep her," he replied.

"You can't look after your own child Devon?" she barked, frustrated with him. They were still married and they were on a six-month reconciliation period ordered by the court due to Devon telling the judge he wanted his marriage and wanted a chance to reconcile. She wanted to punch him in his face when they left the courtroom after the judge agreed to give him the six months and now he was pissing her off again. She had plans for over three weeks to have that weekend off so she could be with Ray and now Devon was tripping.

"Leila why can't you just say where you are going and that

will be that," he said, like it was just that simple.

"You know what, Devon? Forget it okay? You don't have to keep DJ, I'll figure something out," she said and slammed the phone. She was mad and she didn't want to beg Devon for anything. She wanted to cry but didn't let a tear fall. She just wanted to have a weekend not worrying about having her baby with her. She was spending the weekend at Ray's and his place was not baby friendly, so it was not such a good idea to take her ten month-old walking baby over to his non-baby friendly place. She sat there and ignored Devon's back-to-back calls. She didn't have anything to say to him and refused to pick up to hear his irritating ass voice. She called Renee to see if she could keep the baby for her, but since they had planned to close the store that Saturday three weeks ago, she and her husband had plans.

Leila sat there and fought the tears as she contemplated on what she should say to him. She really didn't want to cancel, but she had no choice. She had no friends or real friends she could trust to keep her little one. She didn't want to tell Ray that she couldn't make it, but she was left with no choice, she thought as she dialed his number. She looked over at her little angel and realized she was making the right decision because her little girl was more important. Her heart pounded as she waited for him to pick up.

"Hey beautiful," he said cheerfully.

"Hey what's up?" she said nervously. She didn't want to back out of their romantic weekend, but she had no choice.

"Nothing too much babe, just finishing up dinner," he said, stirring the soup he prepared for them to eat before their main course.

"Um, listen," she said, biting her bottom lip. "I'm not going to be able to make it. Um, Devon is being a jerk and I am afraid I'm going to have to cancel our weekend."

"What, are you serious? You can't be serious," he said, disappointed. "What? What happened?" he asked, not believing what he was hearing. He had pulled all the strings he could to free up a

Saturday and now she called with an *'I can't make it,'* he thought to himself.

"Look Ray I'm sorry, but Devon is tripping and he says he can't take the baby this weekend and I didn't want to call you and cancel, but baby I don't have a sitter for Deja," she said, trying not to cry.

"Well just bring her with you," he said and that was not a good idea, Leila thought.

"I can't Ray. Deja is walking and into everything and your place is not baby safe. It's not Deja-friendly and where would she sleep?" she asked, now even more upset.

"Come on Leila, she can't get hurt over here and she can sleep with us babe," he said, not wanting to take no for an answer.

"Ray come on now, I'd enjoy myself, but there are no toys and you have hardwood floors and sharp end tables and my baby would be miserable," she explained and he leaned against the counter and put his head down. He couldn't believe what he was hearing; after they both had talked about that weekend constantly and were counting down the days.

"Please babe, we can get a hotel suite with carpet or something. Just please tell me that we are still on for this weekend. I cooked dinner for you and I have chilled wine and a bubble bath and candles. I rearranged my entire work week for this weekend, you can't say no," he pleaded and she felt so bad.

"Baby I know and I'm so sorry," she said and that is not what he wanted to hear. He was pissed and wanted to cuss, but he remained calm. He held the phone and didn't speak and she knew from his silence he was upset. She held the phone for a minute or two and then it came to her. "Look baby, why don't you come over here for the weekend?" she asked and it shocked him. He never went to her house before because technically she and Devon were still married and the house was still in both of their names. He never asked or even volunteered to go over to her house.

"Leila I don't think that's a good idea."

"Why not? Devon and I are over and this is where I live. He entertains and has guests at his condo," she expressed, trying to get him to see that it was okay.

"But your name ain't on his condo Leila and technically that's still his house that you live in," he said, not comfortable with her idea.

"Well technically, he doesn't get his mail here and has not lived here since I was three months pregnant with my ten month-old. So he doesn't live here," she snapped.

"Leila baby I would love to come and trust me when I say I do want to see you this weekend, but I wouldn't feel comfortable in his house," he said and Leila didn't push.

"Okay then, I guess I'll see you next week sometime," she said, disappointed too.

"Hold on, it's like that?"

"Like what? I invited you to my home to spend the weekend with me and you said no, so what else is left to say?" she asked, taking off her earrings. She was looking beautiful with her fresh hairdo and make-up and new outfit and it was all for nothing. She looked at her overnight bag and hated she had to unpack it, but Devon was the last man she would ever beg to do something for her.

"I guess you're right," he said, turning off the soup. Their plans were gone. "Well can you at least come have dinner with me?"

"Yeah, I can do that," she said, smiling. There was hope; at least she could see him for a few hours.

"Thank you," he said, relieved he would at least get to see her and not waste the dinner he prepared for them.

"No thank you, just understand I got to bring Deja," she said, reminding him that she would not be alone.

"That's cool. I hope she likes lamb," he said, opening the oven to check on the lamb.

"Naw, but her mommy does," she said, putting her earrings back on.

"So, I'll see you ladies soon."

"Yes, we are on our way," she said and got her baby ready to roll. It was so cold so she bundled the both of them up and headed for the door. She was not happy to see Devon calling her again, so she hit *'Ignore'* and hoped he'd get the hint and stop calling her. By the time she made it over to Ray's, her baby was sleeping and she called him when she was downstairs. He came down to help her and when they got up to his place, he took Deja into his room; Leila followed and took off her coat, hat and sweater.

"She is getting so big Leila and she is beautiful," he commented.

"Thanks, this li'l piggy gets into everything," she said and placed her in the middle of the bed. She wasn't worried because he had a low platform bed and Deja knew how to get off the couch, so she figured she'd be fine. They went to the kitchen and she watched him get the glasses and plates.

"The food smells divine," she said, taking in the aroma.

"Thanks, I hope you enjoy," he said, handing her a glass. "Have a seat," he said and she sat at the little dinner table that he had off the kitchen in the corner. He had candles burning and soft music and Leila wished she was there alone to enjoy the weekend that they had planned. They ate and talked and laughed and he refilled her glass.

"So, why do you always have red wine?" she asked because she preferred white. Red was fine, but white was more her flavor.

"Well my dear red wines are better for your heart and they do not have all the calories that are in white wines, so that is why I usually have red and plus red goes well with beef, red sauces and lamb," he said and got up to clear the table. She was not too impressed because she knew everything he said was true, but he maintained good exercise so the calories would not have interrupted his physique.

"I got you, but white wine tastes better to me," she commented as she got up to help him. They cleaned the kitchen together and settled in the living room. He grabbed her foot and gave her a nice massage and she closed her eyes and enjoyed him. Just when he took her other foot, they heard loud thump and then her baby screaming and Leila launched from the sofa and Ray was right behind her. Her baby was screaming and after Leila examined her, she realized she was more frightened than hurt.

"Baby I'm sorry, I had no idea my bed would be too high," he said nervously and apologetic.

"No Ray, it's not your fault. She just woke up in a strange place, that's all and the fall just scared her. She is not hurt," Leila said and he went into the bathroom to get a cold towel for her head anyway.

"I know, but I hate that she fell," he said, feeling awful.

"Ray, she is fine," Leila said and Deja was no longer crying. She was looking around, trying to figure out where she was.

"I know but-," he tried to say.

"Babe look, she is okay," Leila said and they went into the front. She sat on the couch and Deja wanted to get down, so Leila let her go. Ray was nervous with every step she took and he then made a decision.

"Listen, I wanna be with you this weekend, so if it would be better for your daughter if we went to your place, I'd like to go," he said and Leila smiled.

"Really?"

"Yes, really," he said and kissed her. "Let me grab a few things and then we can go," he said and she smiled. He went into his room, packed a few things and then they got bundled up again and left. They decided it was better for him to follow so she would not have to bring him back on Sunday. She drove with goose bumps all the way home.

XX

"Come on in," she told him as he followed her into the entryway of her huge brick three-leveled home. It was beautifully decorated, he thought as he looked around.

"Wow, Leila your home is amazing," he complimented as she took his coat and headed to the coat closet.

"Thanks, give me a moment and I'll show you around," she said and unbundled her baby. Deja immediately headed for the stairs and began to climb them, headed to her room.

"Leila she is climbing the stairs," he said, not believing his eyes that she was so independent and mobile for such a small child.

"It's cool, she is just going up to her room," Leila said, walking by like it was no big deal. She used to be nervous when Deja went for the stairs, but after a couple weeks of trying to stop her, she gave in and allowed her to explore. She was also surprised when she saw her little body climb all twelve steps and go into her own room. She was almost eleven months and she had the stairs down to a science. "Come, let me show you the rest of the place," she said and he followed. She started on the main floor, showing him her huge gourmet kitchen and spacious family room. He peeped into the two spare bedrooms and admired her formal living and dining room. They headed downstairs into the basement and Ray thought he had walked into heaven when he laid eyes on the finished home theater that she had and he was floored when she told him that she didn't go down there at all.

She showed him the very small office area and spare bathroom and they headed up to the third level. They peeped in on Deja and she was so busy entertaining herself she didn't notice them. After they took a quick look at the hall bathroom, she showed him to her master suite, where they would be retiring for the night and he felt like he was home. The decor overall was lovely and Leila kept a clean home and he was glad he made a decision to go. They went back down to the kitchen and she grabbed a bottle of white wine from her wine cooler.

"White huh?" he said and made himself comfortable at the spacious island.

"Yep, I love it," she said and grabbed a couple of glasses from the cabinet.

"So, did you do all of the decorating?" he asked and she handed him his glass.

"Yep, everything except for the basement. That was all Devon's doing and then he bounced," she said and laughed a little.

"I know it must have been hard. Is that why you don't go down there?"

"No, I'm mostly here by myself with the baby and we don't need HD and surround sound to watch Shrek," she said and he laughed.

"Well I don't know now, a huge flat screen HD set like that would make Esther from Sanford and Son look like America's Next Top Model," he said and she laughed.

"Well I wouldn't know. I've never turned it on."

"Get out," he said, thinking she had to be putting him on.

"Nope, Devon watched it a few times with his pals and not too long after the construction was done, he was done with me," she said and looked away.

"Come on, let's go sit on the sofa," he said, taking her hand. They sat in silence for a few moments and he struck up another conversation.

"I'm so looking forward to getting married and buying a home as beautiful as this and having a couple kids," he said and Leila was surprised to hear that come from him.

"Really, you actually want to get married?"

"Oh yeah," he said and took a swallow of his wine.

"Wow, the idea of me ever being married again is like non-existent."

"Why would you say that?"

"Because I'm not getting any younger, I have a kid and I don't exactly look like America's Next Top Model."

"Please Leila, don't even. You know you are beautiful and there is nothing wrong with the fact that you already have a child and you never know what's in store for your future."

"Yeah, I guess you are right. I just don't want to marry the wrong man again, you know? Devon and I were inseparable once and now it's like I can't remember how good it was when it was good," she said with a look of despair on her face.

"Leila listen that is all behind you. You have to look at what's good in front of you and I'm here with you and I want to make memories with you that you will never have trouble remembering," he said and before she could blink Deja was standing by the side of her leg.

"Hey sweet pea, what's up?" she asked, smiling in her motherly tone.

"Bah, bah, bah," Deja said.

"Bottle? You want your bottle?" Leila asked, getting up and correcting her speech. She was aware that Deja was still small, but she never used baby talk; she only used real words with her.

"Bah, bah," Deja said again and followed Leila into the kitchen. She got her a bottle and sat her on the sofa and ran up to get her nightclothes. She put her on a fresh diaper and got her into her bedclothes and before she was halfway done with her bottle she was sleep. Leila took her upstairs to her nursery and pulled the door up a little. She went back to join Ray and he was up refilling their glasses.

"I could have gotten it for you," she said, taking the glass he handed her.

"No baby, it's cool," he said and followed her back into the family room. She grabbed the remote and turned on some soft music and they sat there and talked a little and mostly just looked at one another. They finished their wine and decided to head up. Ray grabbed his bag and she made sure the door was locked and set the alarm. When she got up, she went into the bathroom and started some water so she could take a bath.

"The remote is here and I'm not sure what you wanna watch, but knock yourself out," she said and handed it to him.

"I wanna watch you," he said and the hairs on the back of her neck stood up.

"Watch me what?" she asked, like she didn't know what he was talking about.

"Take a bath," he said, moving closer to her.

"Really?" she asked, with a sexy smile.

"Yes really," he said and tossed the remote onto the bed. He took her by the hand and led her back into the master bath. He started to undress her and she knew it was going to be one of those nights. She stepped into the tub while the water was still running and laid back to make herself comfortable. He put his hand in the water and then began to rub on her legs and made his way up to her inner thigh and she closed her eyes and allowed him to caress her skin. She tried to remember the last time Devon touched her like that and it was funny because she couldn't. She opened her eyes when she felt his hand touch her breasts. He massaged them and she was so glad she was no longer breast-feeding and her milk had finally dried up to a point that they didn't leak.

She didn't know if it was safe for him to suck on them, but she knew licking them was definitely an option. She took her hand out of the water and touched the back of his head and he smiled.

"You are a lovely woman Leila, inside and out. You have so many qualities that are beneath the exterior of your skin and I wouldn't change one thing about you," he said and it made her blush. The water was full enough for him to turn it off, so he turned off the faucet. She secretly couldn't wait 'til the bubbles rose and covered the ugly stretch marks on her stomach, but after what he just said to her made her feel like a diamond and she decided to put all of her insecurities about herself to the side to enjoy the fine ass ten she had touching her in all the right places. "I'll be right back," he said and stood to get the lighter that he noticed on her nightstand next to a candle. She wondered where he was going, but he was back within a couple seconds. "Here we go," he said, lighting the candles that she had sitting around her tub and on her vanity. He turned out the lights and returned to her side.

"This is nice," she said, giving him a warm smile.

"Yes it is," he said, taking her hand out of the water and kissing her fingertips and it sent chills all over her skin, even though she was in a tub of hot water.

"Ray, you are so perfect and sometimes it amazes me how sweet and kind you are to me. I mean, I would never try to compete with any other woman, but a few weeks ago when we first hooked up, I didn't take you as serious as I do now. I mean, I keep telling myself any moment the camera crew is gonna come out of the woodwork saying, *Ah ha - gotcha*," she said, being honest with him.

"Leila, I understand what you are saying and you know it is a shame or should I say sad for any woman, person or whomever to ever think that they are not good enough or fine enough or sexy enough for someone. I mean, I know that people are attracted to beauty, but when I decided to go into physical fitness a few years ago, I learned early that beauty comes in all shapes, sizes and attitudes.

"I have worked with women who you couldn't get with if you look like Morris Chestnut or Denzel, because they were interested in men with money and looks have absolutely nothing to do with it. I've met not so fine or eye-catching, according to society standards, but was so confident in who they are, no one could convince them that they were not as fine as Halle or Nia Long. I am sorry you felt like me wanting you was a joke or some kind of game - because I see Leila.

"I can also see that you are in this beautiful package, so from now on, please for me, know that I am not all that and nothing or no one is too good for you," he said and her heart pumped a mile a minute. She knew that she was done at the moment with the doubts and insecure thoughts about her weight and body. Devon had done a number on her self-esteem and she still didn't feel pretty enough to be wanted by a man.

Devon used to call her names and tell her she wasn't going nowhere with him looking like a cow. When she was pregnant, she remembered him comparing her to the Good Year Blimp and that stuck out in her mind, every time Ray ever told her she was beautiful. She wanted to believe him so many times, but now she was starting to be convinced. Ray showed her attention, kindness and interest and she was the one with the hang-ups, because Devon had her messed up. Had her convinced that she was not attractive anymore and no one would want her.

"So I can relax?"

"Yes baby I want you to relax," he whispered and went back to exploring her body. He touched, rubbed and massaged every inch that he had access to while she closed her eyes. He rubbed on her clit so easy and smooth 'til she moaned out loud and gasped for air. She didn't want to wet up everything, but she grabbed the back of his head again with her wet hand.

"Aw, aw, aw, aw, baby, aw, my goodness," she whispered,

still trying to catch her breath.

"You liked that baby?" he asked, proud that he had accomplished his quest of helping her to orgasm.

"Oh baby, you know I liked that, you know I did," she said and he stood. He undid his belt and then took off his shirt. He went into her room and came back with his toiletry bag. Leila was out of breath and exhausted from coming so hard and good, she didn't asked him what he was doing.

When she finally opened her eyes, she saw his beautiful body standing before her naked. He opened the shower door and turned on the water and waited for it to warm up before he stepped in. She was enjoying the view of his body in the shower as he lathered up. He was so sexy and fine to her, she had to shake herself back to reality and accept that he was hers. He wanted her and she wanted him even more as she watched the water roll down his perfect chest and tight ass stomach.

He grabbed the bottle of liquid soap again to lather once more and when he began to wash his dick it began to stiffen and her hot spot began to jump again. She knew she should have been bathing, but she began to touch herself. She didn't take her eyes off his dick as he lathered his erection and to her surprise she got another. It was so good she trembled and she whispered the words, "I'm in trouble," and she was glad he didn't hear her. She sat up and grabbed the Bath & Bodyworks bath gel and did her thing so she could get out. She grabbed her robe and went into Devon's drawer of shit that he somehow didn't take with him and got a robe for Ray and took it into the bathroom.

"What's that for?" he asked as he dried his skin.

"It's for you. It's a robe," she said, wondering what he meant.

"I don't need that," he said and she looked at him funny. "And you don't need this one either," he said and pulled her close to him by the belt. He grabbed her face and kissed her so passionately and pushed her robe off her shoulders and it dropped to the floor. He ran his tongue down her neck and quickly went for her nipple.

The sensation of him sucking on them made her moan out loud and her spot was definitely ready to be pleased. The heat between her legs must have warmed up the room because he took her into his strong arms and put her up on the vanity between the two sinks.

He used his fingers first to test her wetness and then he went down and began to lick her. She didn't hold back and let out loud moans and deep breaths. She told him how good he was and how he was making her tight spot feel. She grabbed the back of his head and thought that she had to be dreaming when she felt another one. She couldn't remember ever in her life having three in less than an hour and she thought for sure she was going to pass out.

"Baby, please, please, no more, I'm gonna pass out," she pleaded.

"Naw baby, I'm not done with you yet," he said and Leila almost passed out for real. No man ever spoke to her like that or made her feel wanted like that.

"Give me a minute baby, I promise I'm going to let you have your way with me. I just need a minute to recoup and I need to look in on Deja," she said, coming up with any excuse to be able to get away from him for at least two minutes because he was doing the unthinkable to her and she was falling in love before her divorce was final.

"Okay, but hurry back," he said and planted another wet kiss on her lips.

"I will," she said and inched away from him. She walked out into the hall naked and peeped on her sleeping baby. She knew Deja was sound asleep, but she had to get her second wind. She walked back toward her door and stood outside for a minute and smiled brightly and went back inside to her man. He was in her bed waiting for her and she almost let the image of Devon invade her thoughts until he spoke.

"Come here sexy, so I can get some of that good stuff you got," he said, pulling back the covers and she laughed.

"You are too much," she said as she climbed into bed.

"Aw, you ain't seen nothing yet," he said and gave her the best of the best lovemaking she had ever had in her life. She collapsed on his chest and all she remembered was the kiss he put on her forehead before she was in a deep sleep. The next morning, Deja was up by seven a.m. and Leila did not expect that. She dragged herself out of bed and went downstairs and got her a bottle and tried to make her go back to sleep, but she was up and talking and wanting to get out of her crib.

Leila cringed and went to the hall bathroom to relieve her bladder and then went back into her room and slipped on some sweats and a halter. She got her baby and headed downstairs and got her some eggs and grits. She fed her and before she knew it, it was after noon. She went up and Ray was still sleeping so she didn't bother to wake him. By one, Deja began to get restless and was ready for a nap. She got her down and decided she was going to make herself some breakfast.

XXI

She turned on the music and took out the items she needed for an omelet and made herself a mimosa. She put a few strips of turkey bacon on a pan and put it in the oven and sang along with the music as she diced the vegetables for the omelet. She figured the aroma from the bacon must have waked him because he came down in some shorts and a tank.

"Good morning beautiful," he said and kissed her and she could smell the fresh scent of Crest on his breath.

"Good afternoon handsome," she said and he looked at the digital read out on her microwave.

"Damn girl, you put a brother out," he said and took a sip of her mimosa and frowned. "What's this?" he asked, surprised at the taste.

"It's a mimosa," she said and took her glass out of his hand.

"Oh that's what they taste like?" he asked, taking the glass and trying it again.

"Yep, you've never had a mimosa?" she asked, turning on the burner on the stove.

"No, I have wanted to, but never have," he said, opening the cabinet for a glass.

"Well I love them. Do you want me to make you one too?"

"Sure, I'll have one. Do you need help with anything?" he asked, looking for something to do.

"No, just have a seat and let me cook for you for a change," she said, smiling and he didn't argue. She always went to his loft, so he did most of the cooking.

"Where is Deja?"

"Oh she is napping. That girl got up at seven this morning," she said, pouring the eggs in the pan.

"No way," he said and sipped the drink she fixed him before she started on the omelet.

"Yes way," she said, hoping she got a perfect omelet for Ray. She took the bacon out of the stove and dropped the lever on the four-sliced toaster to toast bagels for the both of them.

"Wow baby, you've been up since seven?" he asked, feeling bad because he slept 'til after one.

"Yeah, but I'm good," she said and flipped a perfect omelet. She added some shredded cheese and grabbed the wisp to get her eggs ready to go into the skillet next. The toaster popped up as she poured her eggs into the frying pan and she took two out and put them on Ray's plate with his omelet and bacon. She had fresh strawberries and cantaloupe on the island for them to have with their breakfast. She put his plate in front of him and went back to flip her omelet and it too was perfect. She grabbed the cream cheese from the fridge and gave him a butter knife.

"No thanks babe," he said, waiting patiently for her to join him.

"What do you mean? Strawberry cream cheese is the bomb," she said and slid her omelet onto her plate and turned off the fire.

"I know, but it is loaded with tons of fat and calories and that stuff is not good for you," he said and Leila paused. She felt uncomfortable again because she loved it and couldn't eat her bagel without it.

"Well Ray, I don't see a little cream cheese blowing away your six pack," she said and he heard the sarcasm in her voice.

"I know that babe and I'm not suggesting that you not enjoy your cream cheese. I just don't touch the stuff," he said and pushed it over to her and for some reason she didn't want to touch it. She felt uncomfortable to eat it in front of him because she imagined him saying something to her like Devon would when he watched her eat things that were no good for her and he would make horrible comments and she knew that would be Ray's next step, so she pushed her plate forward and grabbed her glass.

"What's wrong?" he asked.

"I don't feel like eating anymore," she said and turned away.

"Why? What did I do?" he asked, confused.

"Nothing, at least not yet," she said, getting emotional.

"What? Leila I'm lost. What just happened?"

"You think I'm a pig because I like cream cheese?" she asked and he was wondering what happened to the Leila he just kissed when he came down the steps a few moments ago.

"What baby? What are you talking about? I don't think that. Why would you ask me something like that?"

"Devon used to do that; make a remark about any and every food that I like, as if I wasn't supposed to eat," she said and the tears formed. He knew he had to bring her back to reality and make her aware that he was not Devon.

"Listen Leila, I don't have a problem with you loving cream cheese and if you wanna load up your bagel baby go right ahead. My thoughts of you wanting to have cream cheese on your bagel are far from you being a pig. I am not trying to change you or make you do what I do and if you want the cream cheese knock yourself out babe. And," he said, holding up his finger, "I am not Devon and I know how he ruined your self-esteem and criticized you every chance he had and I'm sorry you had to experience such an awful episode with him, but please recognize that I am Rayshon Johnson and I would never think something so horrible about my lady.

"You are who I chose and to choose you and then think ill shit like that is not who I am, so please eat your food and pack on all the cream cheese you want. I am completely happy with you the way you are," he said and caressed her cheek. Leila did feel a little foolish for comparing him with evil ass Devon, so she did what she intended to do in the beginning - put a load of cream cheese on her bagel and enjoy her breakfast.

They went into the family room to watch a little TV and get comfortable on the sofa, but a few moments later Deja was up. She was ready for lunch and Leila was truly drained, but she went into mommy mode. She got her some macaroni and cheese and heated it up. She took Deja into the family room, but she kept yawning and Ray could see she was exhausted.

"Listen baby, let me take her and feed her and you go up and get a nap."

"No, I'm good," she said and yawned again.

"Come on Leila, you are exhausted babe and I can feed and take care of Deja," he insisted.

"Ray, you don't know how to take care of Deja," she protested.

"Leila, how hard could it be?" he asked, taking Deja from her lap and grabbing the bowl. When Deja didn't cry, Leila felt at ease.

"I am sleepy," she confessed.

"I know, so go up and me and Deja gon' eat our mac and cheese and hang out," he insisted.

"Are you sure, Ray?" she asked, still not convinced.

"Go, go, I got this," he said and she went on upstairs and was sleep before her head hit the pillow good. She woke up and it was three hours later and she couldn't believe she had slept that long. She got up and went to the bathroom and then went downstairs. Ray and the baby were not in the family room and she hoped he hadn't left the house with her baby as she walked over and looked out the window to see if his truck was gone. She called out Ray's name when she saw his truck still parked in the driveway.

He didn't respond, so she figured the only other place they could be was downstairs in the basement. She opened the basement door and then she heard the television and Deja laughing really hard and loud. She went down the steps, wondering what was going on. When she got to the bottom, Ray was carrying Deja around in the air like she was an airplane and Deja was cracking up.

"Hey you two," she said, interrupting their good time.

"Hey look - there's mommy," he said and Deja was still laughing.

"Come here you, are you having fun?" she asked Deja and kissed her on the cheek. "How was she?"

"She was good, we've been having a ball," he said, reaching over to tickle Deja's tummy.

"Why did you come down here?"

"Because this is a cool space and I noticed the PS3, so Deja and I played a little boxing and a little football. We just been hanging out down here, I hope you don't mind?"

"No, not at all and I had no idea that thing was still here or even hooked up, as a matter of fact."

"You mean to tell me you really don't come down here to enjoy any of this?" he said, thinking that was just odd.

"No, I don't, honestly."

"You got a big ass flat screen and these comfy leather recliners and you don't watch movies down here?"

"No Ray, I don't. Why is that so hard to believe?"

"Because this set up is so great and tonight, my dear, your

days of not coming down here and enjoying this home theater are over. We are going to order pizza and get popcorn, candy and stuff I know that I'm gonna regret eating tomorrow and we are going to watch movies. If I had a room like this, I'd only come out for work," he said, admiring the space again. He was impressed with the soundproof walls and state of the art equipment and he knew Devon spent a pretty penny on it and for Leila to not take advantage of a room like that in her own home was a travesty, in his opinion.

"Okay, we need to head to the video store, because I don't have any recent movies," she said with a smile. It felt so good to have a man in her house. She would have done anything he said, as long as he was there. When they got in her truck, they headed to the video store. Since it was cold, Leila and Deja stayed in the truck while Ray went inside to get the movies. She dug around her purse to get her ringing cell phone and her smile faded when she saw that it was Devon.

"Hello," she said, irritated.

"Leila, what in the hell is going on with you?" he yelled.

"What is it Devon? What do you want?" she asked. She was in no mood for his ass and she wished she hadn't answered her phone.

"I called you all damn night and been calling you all day and your phone keep going straight to voicemail - and your cell phone, you just don't bother to answer it?"

"Well Devon, why didn't you use your brain and figure out I didn't want to talk to you?" she said and saw Ray coming out of the store.

"Lei, don't play with me and you know as long as my child is with you, you need to answer your phone."

"Devon, Deja is fine okay? If she were not, I would have called you. Why are you so concerned now when you could have had your child this entire weekend?" she asked and held up one finger when Ray opened the door. She didn't want him to say anything.

"Listen, I would have taken care of her if you would have just told me where you were going," he spat.

"Well Devon that is not your business. So, what do you want now?"

"I want to come and see Deja," he said and that was definitely not a good idea.

"Devon please, don't call me with this *'I wanna see my baby'* crap," she said in disbelief.

"Lei you are starting to piss me off, you know that?"

"Oh well Devon. And I'm not home anyway."

"Where are you?"

"Not home," she spat.

"Not home where?" he yelled. "Where in the hell are you with my child?"

"Devon, you need to calm down and lower your voice. My daughter is with me and she is safe and unharmed."

"And I want to see her, so where are you?"

"You can see her Devon, but it won't be tonight," she told him.

"Like hell it won't!" he yelled.

"Look Devon, did you want anything important?"

"Yes, I want you to bring your ass home and let me see my child."

"No," she said and Ray reached over and touched her hand. They were on their way to pick up the pizza and he could see Devon was upsetting her. "You don't have control or power over me and I'm not going to let you tell me what to do. I am not going to cancel my plans or change my plans to accommodate yo' ass. So, you will see DJ tomorrow," she said, putting down the law.

"You know what Lei? I will see you at the house."

"Well you can wait all night because I won't be home 'til tomorrow," she said, lying. She didn't want Devon to come to her house and see her with Ray.

"Lei, don't fucking play with me. Bring yo' ass home," he said and saw the white Tahoe in the driveway of Leila's house. "Who the fuck does this Tahoe belong to in our driveway?" he asked and Leila was surprised he was at her house.

"Our driveway? You mean my driveway. You live at 2240 Park Avenue, not 404 Langston Place," she said, making it clear that he didn't live with her anymore.

"Lei!" he yelled and Leila knew it was about to be madness.

"No, no, no, Devon. Here's where reality kicks in and hits you in the face. We are no more and I am not with you and you and I do not live together. You moved on when you moved out and now I am moving on. M O V I N G on," she said, spelling it out. She was done and Devon had to know she meant what she said. "So, get your ass away from in front of my house and I will see you tomorrow," she said and hit the "End" button on her phone. Before she could say a word to Ray, it rang and she didn't answer, but Devon began to call her back to back.

"Baby you should answer that and take care of it. I mean, we can't circle for the rest of the night. Once we pick up the pizza, we gon' have to go back and he may still be there," Ray said, pulling into the pizza parking lot.

"I know Ray, but damn. I didn't want to do this tonight. I didn't want you in any situations with me and Devon."

"Well don't worry about me. I am a grown ass man and I know this could get ugly, but believe me, he is not going to step to me like that," he said and undid his seat belt. He went inside to get the pizza and Deja was still sleeping peacefully. Leila held on to her ringing phone and tried to avoid picking up. She thought Devon would just give up and go home, but when they pulled onto her block he was still sitting there parked on the street. She swallowed hard and took a deep breath as Ray pulled into her driveway. She undid her seat belt and looked over her shoulder and saw Devon getting out of his car.

"It's going to be fine," Ray said and she smiled. Deep down she knew it wasn't the truth, but she smiled anyway. She opened her door to get out and Devon quickly approached her truck.

"Lei, we need to talk now," he demanded, grabbing her arm and Ray looked at him like he was crazy but didn't say anything. He decided he'd give Leila a chance to handle it; if things escalated, he was going to have to step in.

"Let me go Devon," she said and snatched away from him.

"Lei," he said, impatiently clenching his teeth.

"Ray, let me see the keys please," she said and he handed them to her. "This is the house key; you can go on inside," she said and he didn't budge.

"Leila can we please?" Devon asked.

"Can we please what Devon?" she asked, turning to him with a serious look on her face. She was tired of him and tired of his controlling ways.

"Look," he said, looking over at Ray. "I just want to get DJ and I'll be on my way," he said, not wanting to provoke Ray.

"Fine, you want your kid, here ya go," she said, handing Deja to him. "I'm sure you have everything you need at your place for her or did you need anything?" she asked, handing him her diaper bag. Devon had everything from milk to clothes and toys at his place, so Leila knew she didn't have to go into the house for anything.

"This is far from being over, believe that," he said and walked away. He put the baby in her car seat and gave Leila an evil look before he got into his car. She and Ray stood there and waited for him to leave before they got the pizza and movies and went inside

"Oh my God, he's an asshole!" Leila yelled as she locked the door. She was so upset and angry she wanted to cry. She was shaking by the time she put the movies on the counter and took off her coat.

Ray looked at her and saw how upset she was and he didn't understand why she was letting Devon get beneath her skin.

"Baby calm down and stop okay? Breathe, come on take a deep breath for me and relax," he said, rubbing her shoulders.

"Why does he live to torture me, huh? What in the fuck does he want from me?" she yelled and began to sob.

"Baby, come on now, shhh," he said, trying to comfort her. He held her tight while she cried. "Please baby, take a breath. Relax and calm down. Don't cry babe. It's not so bad, trust me. Come on, relax and take a deep breath for me. I can't stand to see you cry babe," he said and she began to calm down.

"I'm sorry - I didn't want to get you in the middle of my madness."

"Baby it's okay. Nothing happened. Everything is okay," he said, trying to reassure her that he was cool.

"I know nothing happened, at least not this time. I don't know why he just won't give me the divorce and move on."

"Because you are beautiful, sexy and intelligent, Leila and now he sees that. He sees now that you are worth loving and now he probably regrets leaving you," he said and she didn't believe that those were the reasons Devon was not giving her the divorce. Devon hadn't made her feel worth loving in so long, she forgot how it felt to be wanted, loved and cared for. In such a short time with Ray, he had given her that feeling. He cared for her the way she was and it was not based on physical appearance.

"Ray, I haven't felt love nor have I had a man to love me other than Devon and I know I am a great person with so much love to give, but I don't see how or even if I'll ever experience love again."

"That's where you are so wrong Leila. I adore you and loving you comes so easy because you are so wonderful and if you give me a chance to love you I will love you hard and protect you from pain and all the other bullshit. I'd love to see you carry my babies and care for them like you care for Deja. You don't understand how you have captured my heart in the last couple months and if you want me Leila, I'm right here and I love you and I don't want to be without you," he said and Leila couldn't move.

She knew she and Ray had something good and that love feeling was all over her too, but she never knew he'd fall for her the way she had fallen for him.

"Ray I love you too and I do want you. I knew I was in love with you last night when you packed your overnight bag to come over here and to hear you love me too is like...," she tried to say, but he kissed her.

"I want you to be happy and not worry about Devon and your past. He will not hurt you again and I will deal with him being Deja's dad. He is not going to have you crying and getting upset like this if I can help it. I am going to be here for you and hold your hand and comfort you. So don't let him get you down baby, okay?" he said.

"But Ray, you don't know him. Devon is like a rash that keeps on coming back, no matter how much Cortizone you apply."

"And you can keep scratching that rash or let the Cortizone do its job. Let me make it better. I don't want you to continue to let Devon have this type of power over you."

"You're right, Ray and I, I, I, just don't know how," she stuttered.

"I am here baby, okay? It will get easier," he said and she didn't argue. She just let him hold her for a few moments before they grabbed a couple plates, beers and the pizza. She tried to put Devon out of her mind and went down to join Ray to watch the movies that they rented. She was impressed with the quality of her home theater. It was so nice she declared that they would have movie night at least once a week and they ate all the bad stuff. She and Ray were stuck like glue from that evening on.

XXII

"Devon, why are you dragging this out?" Leila asked. They were with the judge and their attorneys at a hearing and she was so irritated with Devon she wanted to slap the shit out of him.

"First, your honor," he said, trying to get the judge's sympathy. "I love my wife and I'm not ready to just call it quits or throw in the towel. I feel if given another six months, Leila and I can resolve our differences and we can get back to loving each other," he said pathetically.

"Man please…, that's bullshit and you know it!" Leila yelled and the judge didn't like her attitude.

"Motion granted," he said and Leila's mouth opened wider than her eyes that bucked. "I'm giving you six more months Mr. Vampelt and until then this court is adjourned," he said and banged his gravel.

"Judge, please, you can't be serious?" Leila belted with tears in her eyes. She couldn't believe that the judge had actually given it another six months.

"Mrs. Vampelt, please," her attorney said, trying to get her to calm down.

"Walter you are my lawyer - you have to do something. You know that Devon and I are over. We don't need another six minutes to figure that out. I am done with him," she cried and the judge wasn't showing her any favor whatsoever.

"Mrs. Vampelt, if you continue to behave like you have with your outbursts, profanity and clever comments and disrespect my court, six months of reconciliations will be the least of your worries," the judge said and stood to leave. Leila hated him and figured he had to be a miserable old man to allow this madness another six months. She looked away and the tears began to roll down her cheek. Devon was sitting there with a smug look on his face and she wanted to beat the snot out of him, but she knew that wasn't the answer and killing him would only cause her to catch a horrible case.

Everyone but Devon got up to leave and she just sat there and cried. She was so over Devon and their marriage and the sight of him made her sick. Devon got worse and began to drive her crazy once he realized that she and Ray were serious and in love. He gave her a hard time on all occasions because he was now jealous and thought he wanted her back. That was a joke, she told herself, every time he made a ridiculous attempt to make it work.

She got up and got her purse to leave. She tried to walk out without saying a word to Devon, but he spoke up.

"Lei," he said and she paused.

"Devon, don't, okay? Please don't say shit to me," she said and turned to walk away, but he didn't let her.

"Lei, you know I'm not going to just let you go so you can go off and be with this Rayshon. You are mine and you will always be mine," he said with arrogance.

"You know what Devon? You can keep telling yourself that lie. This here is over, done, finished and I am not yours. This belongs to Rayshon Johnson. He does things to me and my body that you, my dear, were never capable of doing and it's okay that you want to drag this divorce out. Just keep in mind that every night your so-called wife is being fucked outta her mind by another man who is not your ass," she spat and walked out. She was at the point where she honestly didn't care what she said to Devon because he was on her nerves day in and day out. If they didn't have a child together, she would have made it her mission to not see him at all.

When she got home, she was tired as hell. Ray had an early client, so he wasn't coming over and she had Deja, so she didn't want to go over to his place, but she needed to see him. Her body wanted to be near him. She called Devon reluctantly so she could get him to take the baby, but of course, he was ignoring her calls.

She figured he was still hot about the comment she made before walking out of the court. She figured he'd call her back when he calmed down. She decided to call it a night, but after she showered and got into bed, she couldn't sleep. She tossed and turned in her bed with the thoughts of the judge giving Devon another stupid six months. She was mad as hell, so she got up and called Ray. She needed him to comfort her and she just had to take her little one with her.

"Hey baby," he said when he picked up.

"Hey babe, I know it's late, but I gotta come over. I don't wanna be alone tonight," she said.

"Sure babe, you know you can," he said. She got her daughter, who was now a year and three months old and grabbed a few items and headed over, to his loft. When she got off the elevator with her baby and bags, she was tired. She knocked and he opened the door and he quickly helped her with the baby and bags.

"You should have called me from downstairs before you lugged all this up by yourself," he said, putting Deja on the sofa.

"You are so right because that little girl is heavy," she said, stepping out of her shoes. Ray sat down and took off Deja's little sweater and gave her a couple of kisses. She laughed and talked to Ray in her baby talk and he knew that she knew who he was and she liked him. Leila went into his room to undress and get comfortable and then she went back to the front and undressed her baby and put on her pajamas. She put her in her playpen that she had set up, which is where she normally slept when they spent the night over Ray's place. She had baby items and other items at his place, so she didn't have to carry so much stuff back and forth. The more items she left, the more his clients had attitudes and frowns. Ray didn't care and ignored their comments and remarks.

Ray laid in his bed and closed his eyes while Leila got the baby to sleep because she was a little cranky and didn't want to go to sleep. Ray tried to stay awake because he wanted to talk to her about the divorce. He waited all day for the verdict, but she didn't call him with any news, so he figured it was something to it. She eased into bed with him and they snuggled close together and he waited a couple moments before he asked.

"So, how did it go?" he asked.

"How did what go?" she asked as if she didn't know what he was talking about. She didn't want to speak the bad news.

"Come on babe, you know what I'm talking about," he said, rubbing her arm softly.

"No, I don't," she said, still playing the role.

"Leila, shit, now you know I'm talking about the hearing with your husband," he said and that kind of hurt her, but she knew she was the one beating around the bush.

"Ray it was awful and I'm honestly mortified about it."

"What happened?" he asked, sitting up and turning on the lamp on the nightstand. She took a deep breath and told him play by play about the horrible episode.

"And the conclusion is he got the six months," she said sadly.

"What? No way…, did you tell that judge that you didn't love him and you had someone else in your life that you love and wanted to start your life over with?" he asked, disappointed.

"Baby, it doesn't work like that and the judge hates me - I know he does. No matter what I said or what my attorney argued, he felt it necessary to give Devon another six stupid months and for nothing because I am not interested in working it out with him."

"No, this is total bullshit. I can't believe this. This cannot be happening."

"I'm afraid it is," she said softly and she tried not to cry again.

"So we have to put our lives on hold for another six months so Devon can walk around feeling good about himself?" he yelled in anger.

"Ray baby, lower your voice please. Deja," she said, pointing over to her sleeping baby in the playpen next to the bed.

"Leila I'm sorry. I'm just so upset and angry about this bullshit," he expressed in a lower tone.

"I know baby. Trust me, that's exactly how I felt today when the judge said that garbage, but we are not on hold. We are still going to be together and continue to love each other. Devon can't stop that," she said and rested her head on his lap.

"I know babe, but I wanted this to be over today because I wanted to give you this," he said, giving her the black velvet box he took from his nightstand drawer.

"What's this?" she asked, sitting up. She opened the box and it was the most beautiful engagement ring she ever remembered seeing. "No, no, no, no way, Ray, no," she said, looking at the ring. "You can't be serious, no way can you be serious," she said, holding he box.

"I'm so serious Leila and I couldn't wait another day to ask you," he said and she turned to him. Her eyes welled up and she was speechless. "I love you and you are my match. You are my perfect fit. You and that little girl mean so much to me and I wanna be with you and have a family. I want to take care of you two."

"Ray, I don't know what to say. I never expected something like this," she said, not able to take her eyes off the ring.

"Do you love me Leila?" he asked, turning her to face him.

"Yes I love you. I adore you and I want to give you all of me. I wanna spent the rest of my days with you, giving you all the love and affection that you have given me. You helped me to get back to me and you helped me to see who I am and only love could make a person do for someone what you have done for me. I've never felt sexier or more wanted or more special or more loved by anyone and I am honored that you love me this much," she said, holding up the ring. "I would love to marry you Mr. Johnson, yes, yes, yes. My answer is yes," she said and he held her tight. As soon as he let go, she let him put the ring on her finger.

She was so happy at that moment and she didn't care one bit about the six-month period that she had to be stuck with Devon's last name because she could see and be with Ray as much as she wanted. She belonged to Ray, not Devon and she decided she wasn't going to let Devon get to her or get under her skin. She made up her mind that she was going to be as pleasant as possible and pray that the judge would give her what she wanted on their next court date.

XXIII

"Devon, what do you want me to say?" Leila asked impatiently.

"I want you to say that you love me and there is a chance for us," he pleaded and she wanted to laugh.

"Devon, I can't say that because I don't love you and there is no chance for us," she said again. She had told him that over a dozen times.

"Why Lei? Why can't you just try?"

"Devon, you know we have talked and talked about this. We have gone back and forth with this and I don't want to take this trip down memory lane and I'm sure you don't want to either. You abandoned me when I was pregnant with your child. You left me too, too many nights crying my eyeballs out. The night I went into labor, you ignored my back-to-back calls when I was terrified and didn't know what to do.

"I had to call a friend to come and get me to get me to the hospital. You lied to me in the hospital on the night of your daughter's birth that you would come home and work things out. You never came home and I got over the fake promise and lies that you told me, so why, Devon? For the love of God, why can't you let me go and give me the divorce? You didn't want me then, but '*now you wanna come back*' Devon, please give me an answer?"

"Because I love you Leila and I love my child. I have changed and this is no gimmick, no lies, nor fake promises. I love you and I want my marriage. I want one final chance to show you that I'm ready to make it right. I want us to work Leila, so please reconsider and give us a chance to start over."

"Why now Devon? Because I'm not so disgusting to look at anymore or because you know someone else loves me?" she snapped.

"He doesn't love you Leila," he said, like she was nuts. The tone in his voice made it obvious to Leila that he didn't think she was capable of being loved by someone.

"What? You don't know anything about him. You don't know shit about us and you don't have a clue what loving me is about. All you were concerned about was the little Barbie doll, Michelle that you wanted over me and you couldn't love me for who I am, so you just assume Ray doesn't love me either. Why don't you just give me the divorce Devon, so you and I can move on?" she pleaded.

"Because Michelle will never measure up to you Leila," he said being honest.

"What, she can't seem to pour her heart into you and put herself to the side and give you all you need Devon? She can't give you 200% of what you need like I did for years - and you gave me the finger?"

"Lei please, you were the best woman I've ever had and everything about you was good. You were so loving, sensitive, kind and you loved me with everything," he said and her eyes welled. "And I want that again and I need that again," Devon said and she thought back to how she used to do everything for him. She took care of him like a wife was supposed to, but he stopped taking care of her.

"Look Devon, I know how you feel because I have been in your shoes. When I begged you and begged you to work things out and come home and give our marriage a chance, you didn't do that for me. You drove me away Devon. You pushed and pushed and lied and made empty promises and I, I, I don't wanna be married to you anymore, please…, please…, please, tell me why you won't give a divorce?"

"Because I can't, I can't, I don't want to let you go. I can't let you go. I was wrong, Lei, I was a horrible husband and I want to make it up to you. I want our marriage back. I want you back, you are my wife and I want to come back," he cried.

"You don't have me anymore Devon," she said and he was quiet. He put his head down and she looked up at the ceiling to keep from crying.

"Lei, I understand that I hurt you and I made a huge mistake, but I love you so much baby and you can't tell me that you don't love me anymore. I won't accept that," he said with his watery eyes.

"Devon please," she said, not wanting to be cold. As much as he hurt her, she didn't like seeing him in so much pain.

"Leila you want me to beg? I'm begging you. Please, can you give us another try?" he pleaded and she felt for him, but her mind was made up. She was engaged to another man and there was absolutely no chance for her and Devon.

"Devon, I'm sorry. There is nothing else to discuss," she said and went upstairs and left him down on the sofa crying. She sat on her ottoman and cried for the both of them. She prayed and asked God to help the both of them. She prayed for him to accept her decision and just go sign the papers and give her the divorce. She wanted to marry Ray, but that wasn't possible being married. She just had to wait and see if Devon would do what she knew he knew was the right thing to do, but it wasn't going to happen that day and she wasn't sure if he was going to give in at all.

XXIV

"Hold on," Ray said, rushing to the door. It was two a.m. and he wondered who was knocking on his door at that time of morning. He turned on the lamp on the end table and looked through the peephole. "You gotta be kidding me," he said, when he saw Katrina on the other side of the door. He hesitated and took a deep breath before he opened the door.

"Hey," she said softly.

"What do you mean *'hey,'* and what are you doing here at this hour Kat?" he asked, afraid to even hear her answer.

"Well I wanted to say thanks for helping me. You helped save my job and I found a spot and ...," she said, standing there feeling weird. "Can I come in?" she asked and he wanted to say no, but he was a gentleman.

"Sure, but you can't stay long," he said and she came in. He sat in the chair and she sat on the sofa. Ray had pictures of Leila and Deja at his loft and Katrina noticed the photos of them on the coffee table.

"Wow, who's the beautiful little girl?" she asked, as if Leila were not in the picture too.

"That is Deja, my fiancée's daughter," he said, looking at the beautiful picture of the both of them.

"Wow, her baby is gorgeous," she said, not complimenting Leila.

"Yeah, she looks so much like her beautiful mom," he said and Katrina didn't comment or agree. "So, why are you here Kat?"

"Well like I said, I wanted to say thanks," she said, looking around and noticing more photos of Leila and that made her jealous; she thought she wasn't pretty enough to be one of Ray's women, but she didn't say anything.

"Okay, you're welcome, now why are you really here?" he asked and she stood.

"Ray don't be so suspicious. I wanted to give you a proper thank you and I wanted to do it in person," she said, moving over to a wall unit, examining Leila's picture more closely. She unzipped her jacked and took it off, revealing the sexy low cut top she was wearing. She sat down and gave him a sexy look, hoping her plans of getting him back would work that time.

"What are you doing Kat?" he asked, referring to the sexy top and eye contact she was giving him. "I am engaged and I'm happy," he said, hoping she'd get a clue.

"So, this is the woman you are planning to marry?" she asked, picking up the picture from the coffee table.

"Yes, that's Leila."

"Wow, you've changed," she said, putting the picture back.

"Changed how?" he asked, curious to know what she meant.

"Well you know…, your taste in women. I never pictured you with a big girl," she said, putting it bluntly.

"You don't know me like you thought you did and my woman is a full figured queen. Big girl, thick sista, plus size or whatever you want to call it, she is my superstar and I share a life with her that I know I wouldn't have had with you because you, my dear cheated, so that didn't happen," he said, bringing her back to reality. Who was she to talk about anyone when her shit wasn't all that?

"You know…, you're right. I fucked up and I made a lot of horrible choices that caused me a hell of a lot of grief, but you know what? I'm finally at the point in my life where I can own up to my bullshit. Ray, hurting you was one of my biggest mistakes and I'm sorry," she said, sitting on the edge of the sofa. "I know I can't change my past, but I have control of my future and my future would not be worth living without you in it," she said and Ray wanted to laugh in her face. He didn't have a future or anything with Katrina and he preferred to never see her again.

"Kat, you got to be kidding me," he said, shaking his head in astonishment.

"No, I'm not kidding Ray. I'm here to ask you to give me another chance," she said with a straight face and he couldn't believe what he was hearing.

"You may wanna change your brand of crack or get you a new dealer," he said, fighting the urge to laugh.

"I'm not on drugs Rayshon and I am dead serious. You were the best thing that ever happened to me and I've never stopped loving you. I think about you and us all the time and I would like to start over and be the woman that I should have been back then for you. I'm older and wiser and smarter and I am ready to love you the way you deserve to be loved."

"Okay Kat, since you are not high or taking any drugs you must be plain old crazy. I just told you five minutes ago that I am engaged. I am in love with this woman," he said, pointing to the picture on the coffee table. "So, how does your brain tell you to open your mouth and say things about us getting back together?"

"My heart is what tells me to speak. If I don't open my mouth and express to you how much I love you and how much I want us to be together, how would you know?"

"Well now that I know, the answer is no. I don't know who you think you are or what you take me for, but you just can't walk back into my life and just tell me now you want to act right and I'm supposed to just drop everything and say '*Ok, Kat lets pick up where we left off...*' no, it doesn't work like that. *Now you wanna come back* after all the pain you put me through? No Kat, no."

"Why not, Ray? Because of her?" she said, pointing to Leila's picture.

"Yes, because of her. What are you talking about?" he asked, looking at her like she was crazy. "She and I are engaged," he said because she was beginning to irritate him.

"You will never love another woman like you loved me. No way do you have the passion, the emotions or the happiness you had with me with her, do you?"

"You know Kat, I don't," he said and she smiled with confidence. "I have more love, more passion and more happiness with her than I had with you. Leila has this power over me, sorta like a love spell and that I never had with you," he said and she was speechless. "And you know what else? Leila is honest and I can rest easy at night knowing that our love is so strong that she is not off somewhere sharing my goods with some other cat. Something I couldn't say about you," he said and Katrina sat there and the tears welled in her eyes.

"You are right Ray. I was an unfaithful, lying bitch and trust me I've paid for my mistakes. I know that I messed our thing up and I'm sorry," she said and turned her head. She put her feet up and began to sob. He let her cry without saying anything. After a while, she had fallen to sleep and Ray got her a blanket. He didn't want her to stay, but it was late. He went into his room and wondered how he allowed her to sleep on his sofa again.

XXV

The next morning, Christa showed up about ten minutes late and Ray was hoping she'd not show. Katrina was still sleeping on the sofa and Christa saw her and waited 'til she got upstairs before she asked.

"So, what's up with your guest on the couch?" she asked, mid sit up.

"Why are you always minding my business?" he asked, wondering why she even asked.

"Well Ray, you do know that I am not the kinda person not to say what's on my mind and that chick on the couch doesn't look anything like Leila, I'm nosy; so I asked."

"Well Miss Honest, she is an old friend," he said, leaving it at that.

"Wow, she is a pretty old friend. Does your woman know this old pretty friend is on your couch?" she asked as she finished her last sit up.

"Christa please, why can't you come and enjoy your workout without asking a million questions or talking about folks' business?" he asked and she paused before she spoke.

"Well I don't know Ray. I'm sorry," she said, putting her head down. She had absolutely nothing important in her life to be excited about or 100% happy about, so she lived to be in other folks' business.

"Look, I gotta get ready for my next client," he said, grabbing the sweaty towel from the floor and tossing it in the hamper. He continued to wipe down everything and Christa walked down the steps without a bye. When Katrina heard the door shut, she jumped. She got up and went to the bathroom and smiled at her reflection in the mirror. She had managed to lay her head in Ray's loft that night and didn't have to sleep in her car. She had three more nights to find a place to rest her head 'til her apartment was ready to move in.

She finally managed to get back on her feet, but all her cash went on deposits and utilities. She had a few dollars for gas and she had to get groceries when she got into her apartment and she had no money for a hotel room. She just had to bide her time for a couple more days and she hoped to do that at Ray's place. She smiled when she saw things were still in the places they were before and it felt like old times. After she freshened up, she went into the kitchen and realized Ray was upstairs with his next client.

She opened the fridge and grabbed the juice and toasted a bagel. She looked at the clock, noticed Ray would be another forty-five minutes, so she ran down and got her bag from her car. She cringed at all the pictures of Leila around Ray's loft and wished he was still single, not engaged. She went into Ray's master bedroom to shower instead of going to the hall shower. She wanted space to be able to shave her legs and enjoy her shower. She got out and wrapped a towel around her body and went into his room to lotion up. The music was still going upstairs, so he was still working, so she took her time. She wanted him to get a look at her body in the towel, so she didn't bother getting dressed.

When Ray was done and he came down and let Patricia out, he looked around for Katrina and he was pissed to find her in his master bedroom. "What are you doing?" he asked her.

"Putting on lotion," she said, being a smart ass.

"I can see the obvious Kat. What are you doing in my room?

You know there is a shower in the other bathroom."

"I know, but this one is so much bigger," she said, moving around like she was in her own house.

"Listen Kat, you should not have just come into my room and used my shower," he said, aggravated with her, then he paused to keep from going off because he had another client knocking at the door. "Look, just hurry," he said and went for the door. He went upstairs and got started with his seven a.m. and Katrina didn't change her pace and was in no hurry to get dressed. She began to snoop and smile to see Ray still used condoms. At least he wasn't trying to make babies with Leila, she thought to herself. She was stepping into her thongs and she heard the door. She grabbed the towel and went to answer it. She went up on her tiptoes and looked through the peephole and her eyes lit up when she saw Leila. She tossed her hair and opened the door in the towel and the smile faded from Leila's face.

"Can I help you?" Katrina asked, blocking the door.

"Hi, I'm Leila. Is Ray in?"

"Yes, but he is busy," she said, still blocking the entryway. Leila wanted to push past her, but she didn't know what was going on. She had never seen Katrina before and why would a new client be in a towel?

"Well I'm his fiancée, so would you mind?" she asked, trying to move forward, but Katrina didn't budge.

"Listen Leila, I know this maybe a little awkward and I don't think I should be the one to tell you, but I'm Katrina. I'm not sure if Ray ever mentioned me, but we were engaged once. We recently started talking again and you know how it goes…, we are working on getting back together," she said, making it obvious that she was standing in a towel due to sexual reasons. Leila could have fainted, but she played it cool and backed up. "So, Ray will call you soon," she said and Leila didn't say a word. She knew Katrina wasn't lying about being his ex fiancée because Ray told her all about her, but them getting back together was fanatical.

She didn't continue to carry on any more conversation with Katrina because she knew it may have been a brawl if she would have said what she wanted to say. She just turned and headed for the elevator. She sat in her truck and began to sob. She called his cell and of course, it went straight to his voicemail because he was with a client. Leila knew he would be in a session when she went, but she had to get a bag with price tags and a few other items for the store from his place before she opened that morning.

She was in tears and wondered why Ray would hook up with Katrina just like that without any warning or mention that he was thinking about it. Katrina was gorgeous, for one and Leila figured she successfully seduced him with her flawless body and the thought of her plus sized frame was the last thing Ray thought about when he decided to get back with her.

XXVI

She drove to her store, trying to get her thoughts together because she was caught off guard by Katrina and wished she had handled the situation differently. She wished she would have pushed her way in and ran up the steps and confronted Ray instead of allowing Katrina to keep her out in the hall. She wondered why he didn't just tell her instead of cheating on her. Not a single sign was given that he was even considering hooking up with his ex. She went inside of her store in a daze. She cried up until the moment she opened the store and her first customer came in.

She worked in slow motion and was so happy to see her employee, Nicki walk through the door. She had to get inside of her office so she could let the tears she had been fighting all morning out. "Hey, Nicki, I'm so glad you're here. I got a ton of papers on my desk that I need to go through," she said.

"Okay, I'll be fine. I will let you know if we get busy," she said putting her purse and keys down under the counter. Leila went into her office, sat behind the desk and the tears started. She reached for her phone and tried to call him again, but she got the voicemail. She put the phone down and it rang. When she saw it was Devon, she dried her eyes and took a deep breath. She didn't want to talk to him, but he had Deja, so she had to take his call.

"Hello," she said softly.

"Hey Lei, what's going on?"

"Work, Devon. I'm at the store. What do you need?" she asked impatiently.

"Nothing, I was just calling to see what you were doing for lunch. DJ wanted to treat you," he said, being nice and she hated him being nice.

"So, when did DJ get a job or earn money to be able to treat me to lunch?" she asked smartly.

"Well Deja gets by on her good looks," he joked and that made her angry.

"Listen, my daughter is not going to be some beautiful hottie that gets by on her looks. Don't even think of planting that garbage in my daughter's head," she snapped.

"Hold on Lei, I was only joking. What's wrong with you?" he asked, wondering why she was going off.

"I'm sorry Devon, I'm just tired and frustrated," she said, sitting on the edge of her desk.

"It's more than that," he said because he knew her and he could tell by her tone that she was on the brink of crying. "Leila, baby what's bothering you?"

"Nothing Devon, okay? I just can't do lunch with you guys today okay?" she said, holding back the tears.

"Why not?"

"I got a lot going on today and I'm not going to be able to break free for lunch," she said, hoping he didn't push anymore.

"Okay, we will see you later then," he said and Leila was happy to get off the phone. She tried Ray again and got his voicemail. She dialed his house phone and froze when Katrina answered. She was so shocked to hear her voice she just hung up. Even she didn't answer his phone and they were supposed to be engaged. Her mind went crazy and she was in no shape to be at work.

"Nicki, I got to go okay? My head is banging in the worst way and I have to go home. Do you think you can handle the store alone 'til Renee comes?"

"Sure, it's kinda slow anyway. You go on home. I can manage," Nicki said and Leila was relieved. She had never left Nicki alone, but she had no choice.

"Call me if you have any questions, okay?" she told her after she came from the office with her purse and keys.

"I will..., feel better," she said.

"Thanks," Leila said and walked out to her truck. As soon as she started the engine, she began to cry again. She managed to make it home without crashing and went straight to her wine cooler. She poured herself a glass and hit the power to turn on the music. She sang along with Rihanna, "Take a Bow," for a moment and then called Ray again. She tried to catch him at the top of the hour before he got started on his next client, but she got voicemail and then the answering machine. She threw her phone and after crying her eyes out and two more glasses of wine, she dozed off.

The ringing phone woke her up and she got up to get her phone from the loveseat where it landed when she tossed it. She paused and held her breath when she saw it was Ray.

XXVII

"Kat, you are going to have to go," Ray told her after he let his last client out.

"Excuse me?" she asked, looking crazy.

"'Excuse me? What's *'excuse me?'* You been here all damn day and I've been so busy that I couldn't tell you to bounce, so now you gotta roll."

"Why? Are you expecting someone and don't want me to be here?" she asked and sipped her drink.

"No, you just have to leave. We are not tight, close or cool, so you have to go," he said and went into the kitchen for a bottle of water.

"Oh so you are putting me out?"

"Yes, if that's what you want to call it. You have chilled here all day. You have showered, ate, lounged and now you drinking mixed drinks and you are not about to be too drunk to drive, so finish your little drink and go on," he said, putting his foot down. He was not going to let her spend another night. "I have a woman and she would not like you hanging out over here like we are roomies."

"Oh yeah, she came by this morning," she casually mentioned, like it was no big deal.

"Who came by where?" Ray asked with his brow arched and head tilted. He knew damn well Leila didn't come by and see her there without her letting him know she was there.

"Leila…, her," she said, pointing to Leila's photo.

"When…?" he yelled, approaching her slowly. He had never hit a woman, but Katrina was going to be the first to be slapped by him.

"Oh um, about seven-thirtyish," she said and took a drink of her cocktail and he remembered that was around the time he was with Angela and he had just had words with Kat for using his shower after he let Patricia out.

"Katrina, tell me you didn't go to my fucking door in a motherfucking bath towel?" he asked, praying that she had on some clothes.

"Well Ray, I heard the door and I answered it. I didn't know it would be her."

"In a towel? In a towel, Katrina? Why didn't you come and get me? Why didn't you let her in?" he yelled and now he was standing over her, ready to yank her ass.

"Well Ray, you were upstairs with your client and when she saw me, she just left. She didn't ask to come in. I just recognized her from her pictures," she said, lying and took another sip.

"Oh shit Katrina, what in the hell is wrong with you?" he yelled.

"What Ray? And why are you yelling? I didn't do anything," she said, like she was clueless and dumber than a sack of rocks.

"You know what? Get up," he said, taking her drink out of her hand and grabbing her arm. "You get your things and get out of my house," he said, releasing her arm with a slight push. He went into the kitchen and poured out her drink and wondered why she was still standing there, looking stupid. "Katrina, I'm not fucking around. Get yo' shit and get the hell out!" he yelled, walking around collecting her personal items that she had placed around his loft.

"Ray come on now, don't just throw me out. I didn't do anything," she pleaded because she had nowhere else to go. She needed to try and stay there a couple more nights.

"Kat this is not an optional request. You have no idea that you are crazy and if you did anything to mess things up with me and my lady, I promise you…," he said, getting in her face. He was about to threaten her, but it didn't matter; he just wanted her out.

"Fine Ray fine, I'll leave; just let me get the rest of my things," she said and he sat on the sofa. He put his hands on the top of his head and wondered how he managed to allow Katrina to get her way with him again. He was so done with her and he vowed if she ever came knocking at his door again he would never let her in again.

She went into his room to get the rest of her stuff. She looked around and decided she'd leave some evidence behind to prove her lie of them sleeping together. She pulled the covers back and stuffed a pair of red-laced thongs between the headboard and mattress. She took one of the pillows, put her face in it and rubbed her lips across it. She put it back with the clean side facing upwards. She took off an earring and put it on the floor right by the nightstand and bed. She laid her little pinky ring near the phone on his nightstand and then she smiled.

If Leila was coming over that night, she was going to find at least one or two of her planted items, she thought, as she walked out of his room.

"I'm gone," she said, standing near the door.

"Bye," he said and didn't look up. As soon as she was on the other side of the door, he called Leila.

"What?" she said when she picked up the phone.

"Leila baby, please tell me that you don't believe whatever she told you this morning?" he said because he knew Katrina said something.

"Rayshon, tell me how am I supposed to think anything other than what that tramp said? She came to the door in a fucking towel Rayshon, with wet hair. She had an evil smirk on her face and she was guarding the entryway like she was the mistress of the house and you come calling me damn near eleven hours later!" Leila spat.

"Baby, I promise you that nothing happened between me and Katrina. Whatever she told you, I promise you were lies. I am just now calling you babe, because I have had back-to-back appointments. I didn't get a lunch today because Royce, one of my Thursday clients, needed to get in because he going out of town or some shit, but nothing happened," he said, being honest. He did not call Leila too much during the day because he usually did not have time, but once he had a thirty-minute lunch, or free time he would call her.

"Whatever Rayshon, why was the trick there in the first place if nothing is going on? Why was she in a damn towel then Rayshon? Why would she not let me in, even after I told her who I was? Why would she lie and say that you guys were working on getting back together Ray? Why would she do that?"

"She said that? No, baby that is not what happened."

"Why was she there Rayshon?" Leila asked, crying and he could tell. He was not the one to lie, so he told her the truth.

"Listen babe, a few months back, when I told you I had a friend in trouble, it was Katrina. She had lost her mom and had some issues and didn't have a place to go. I helped her out and she came by last night just to say thanks," he said, trying to explain.

"Last night. You let her spend the fucking night Rayshon? That tramp slept over last night?" she asked, now even more upset.

"Yes Leila, but it wasn't like you think. She slept on the sofa. I didn't touch that woman. When you came, I was upstairs with Angela and I guess that's when she used the shower. I didn't know she was showering, for one and she didn't tell me you came by until about ten minutes ago," and the more he talked, the worse things got.

"Oh so not only did she spend the night, she has been chilling at your house all day? That's why she answered the phone when I called."

"She answered my phone, too?" he asked, shocked.

"Oh yeah, so now that I have heard your story, leave me alone," she said and hung up. He called her back, back to back, but she kept hitting "Ignore." She sat there and sobbed and her phone rang again and she was about to hit *"Ignore,"* but it was Devon.

"Hello," she said and she didn't sound good.

"Lei, what's wrong?" he asked immediately with concern.

"Devon I'm sick, okay? I really don't feel well. Can you manage DJ one more night please?" she said, too embarrassed to tell him the truth.

"What is it baby? You sound horrible."

"Devon I know, so can you please, please keep Deja?" she cried.

"Yeah sure, sure. Are you going to be alright? Are you sure you don't want me to come over?"

"No I'm not sure, I do need you," she cried. "I need you to come home," she cried. "I need you home."

"I'm on my way," Devon said and didn't hesitate to rush to her side. He was glad to go to her rescue. She sobbed until Devon made it. She faked having a horrible headache and Devon knew she was having man trouble, but he didn't say anything. He rubbed her back, held her and let her sob. She finally fell asleep in his arms and he wondered what Rayshon had done to her to hurt her so bad.

XXVIII

That night Ray couldn't fall asleep. He was so upset about what went down with him and Leila. He was so pissed at himself for letting Katrina in and not kicking her ass out that morning. He knew if he saw her, he'd kill her ass for sure. How did she manage to hurt him again? Not that she was breaking his heart; she was sabotaging his relationship with the woman he loved. If he lost Leila over that bullshit, he knew for sure he'd go insane. He laid on the sofa and flipped through the channels, looking for something to watch.

After he prayed and called Leila for another thirty minutes straight, he fell asleep. The next morning, the knocking at the door woke him up and he jerked out of his sleep. He realized he had overslept and didn't hear the alarm from his bedroom. He got up, went to the door and told Sonja to go up, get started on the treadmill and he'd be with her shortly. He hurried and brushed his teeth and washed his face. He threw on his gear and ran up.

After a few more sessions, it was Leila's time and he knew damn well she wasn't coming. He never dated his clients, but Leila was his exception. They didn't work out the traditional way; they work out in other ways. He spent that hour making her feel good. Since her appointment was at eleven and his lunch was sometimes at noon, they had an hour and a half to take a bath together, massage each other, or just sit around and they loved it.

He was in the kitchen, he heard the knock at the door and he hurried to open it. He was pleasantly surprised when he saw her.

"Hey, come on in," he said, moving aside.

"I'm not staying; I just came to get my things for the store," she said, walking past him. She had too many items over there, but she had to get the things she needed for her store.

"Listen baby, please wait," he said, following behind her. She was not listening to him; she just wanted to get her bags. "Stop Lei, stop okay," he yelled to get her to pay him attention. She paused and looked down because she didn't want to look at him.

"Ray please, I just need my things for my store okay?" she said, trying to avoid talking to him.

"Leila, nothing happened okay?"

"Save it Ray, okay? Just save it," she said and the tears filled her eyes.

"Baby, please listen to me. I would never do that to you. I love you Leila. Baby, nothing happened. I would never do anything to hurt you," he said, grabbing her.

"No Ray, I thought you would never do anything to hurt me and you did and I know what I saw," she cried and it ate him up.

"Leila, she slept on the fucking sofa. I made a mistake, baby and the only mistake was letting her into my home. Trying to be nice to that bitch is causing me problems with you Lei and I am sorry for letting Katrina in this house that was my mistake. Babe, I swear that I didn't touch that woman. You know me babe, you know me. There are women in and out of here every day, so why would I go back to Katrina baby? Come on, please think. She is an evil lying...," he wanted to continue, but calling her names wasn't going to help his situation. He just wanted to get through to Leila.

"Baby please, come on now. Look at me," he said, lifting her head. "I only want you. I love you and there is no woman that can come up in here and replace you. I would never lie to you. She was here and yes, she spent the night, but not with me. I love you Leila, I want you," he said and kissed her. She wanted to resist him, but she loved him so much. He sounded so sincere and she wanted to believe him.

"Ray why would she stand there and make that shit up?" she asked, trying to be sure.

"Leila, that woman is twisted. She sat here and examined your pictures and I told her how you were so much better for me and how much more of a relationship I have with you than I had with her. She knew about you. I didn't hide your pictures; she knew the truth babe, I guess she was just jealous, I don't know. No way you can look me in the eyes and tell me that you believe that I would hurt you in anyway," had he said and she knew he was right. She trusted Ray and loved him, so she relaxed her tensed position and let him kiss her again.

They ended up in his bed and he pulled at her clothes as if he were desperate to please her. He sucked her nipples so hard and good and she moaned loud to let him know that he was making her feel good. Her body exploded from the passionate love he gave her and before they knew it, their time was up. He had to shower quickly and she just laid there.

She rolled over and grabbed the pillow and she saw the little piece of red lace sticking out from the head of the bed. She was still smiling, but it began to fade when she pulled out the laced thong that Katrina left planted. A fretful look came upon her face and she sat up. She noticed the smeared lipstick on the pillow that she was just holding and she leaped out of bed.

"Ray, you are a fucking liar!" she yelled and he turned off the water.

"What?" he asked, stepping out of the shower to hear what she said.

"You are a fucking liar! I hate you!" she yelled and the tears formed. "You stood there and lied to me," she cried.

"Leila baby, what's wrong? What are you talking about?"

"These," she said and threw the thong in his face and it hit the floor.

"What is this?" he asked as he bent over and picked them up. "Where did these come from?" he asked, confused. He had never seen them in his life.

"I can't fucking believe you!" she yelled and went back into his room to get dressed. She was looking around his room for her clothes and saw the shiny little earring on the floor by the nightstand.

"Lei please, baby, wait. Where did you get these? Kat must have dropped these. I don't know?" he said, confused.

"Oh yeah, she dropped them stuffed between your headboard and did she drop this?" she said, throwing the earring on the bed. "Oh yeah and is this the pillow she had her face in when you were hitting it from the back?" she yelled and Ray was speechless. He knew Kat did that shit on purpose, but he knew he couldn't get out of that situation. Katrina had fucked him real good, he thought, as he stood there naked, dripping water on the floor.

"Leila baby, Katrina did all of this garbage yesterday. I didn't even sleep in here last night. I slept on the sofa. Do you think I'd get up and fix my bed and not notice a pair of thongs and soiled pillow case and the earring?" he said and she wasn't trying to hear him. She dressed quickly and stuffed her panties and bra in her purse as he followed her into the living room. "Leila," he said and she went over to get her bags for the store. "Lei, baby," he said and she keep moving. "Leila," he said, blocking her path.

"Move Ray, I will come by this weekend for the rest of my things. It's over. You are a liar," she said and moved around his naked body. She snatched the door open and his twelve thirty was about to knock.

"Oh hi Mia, he's all yours," she said and she saw him naked. She covered her mouth at the sight of him and he ran into his room.

XXIX

Leila got into to her truck, heated and heartbroken. She drove in circles, confused and hurt. She didn't want to believe what just happened, but it was obvious Rayshon Johnson was the two timing, lying ass dog that played her. She let him play her and now she knew there was no chance for them to get back together. He lied and now she realized he could have been lying to her from the very beginning about everything, his clients, the women and the whole nine. Christa may have had him, hell - who knows, she thought, as she pulled into her driveway.

She was a mess and she was more irritated from the scent of their lovemaking being on her body. She undressed and got into the shower and wept as she washed. She cursed him, yelled and cried and by the time she was done with her shower, she had a banging head-ache. She had to talk to someone, so she called Renee. Renee was with a customer, so she had to call Leila back and that's when she heard Devon pull into the driveway. She ran to the bathroom and washed her face, but her swollen red eyes could not conceal she was in pain.

She let them in, picked up her baby and held her tight. She kissed her ten times before putting her down.

"Hey, I brought your favorite Chinese food. Are you feeling better today?" Devon asked as he followed her into the kitchen

"I'm fine," she said, not wanting to talk to him. She hated him being so nice to her and so concerned.

"Well you don't look fine," he said, washing his hands at the sink. "Sit down and I'll fix you and DJ a plate."

"Devon I can do it," she said.

"Lei sit down, okay?" he said and she didn't argue. She put Deja in her high chair and she sat. She picked over her food and tried to make it without shedding a tear in front of Devon.

"Look, I'm not too hungry. I'm going upstairs," she said and Devon didn't argue. She went into her room and got into bed and just let the tears drop. About an hour, later Devon came up.

"Lei are you sleeping?" he asked.

"No," she said soft and sadly.

"What did he do to you?" Devon asked, now wanting to know.

"Devon please, I don't want to talk right now," she said and he didn't push. He pulled the door up and left her alone. A few moments later, Renee called her back.

"Hey girl, what's going on?" Renee asked.

"Oh Renee, my life is so fucked up," she said and Renee could hear the pain in her voice.

"What happened Leila? What's wrong?"

"Everything," Leila said, crying. She paused for a few moments and Renee just held the phone to give her time to say what it was. "Ray cheated on me with his ex."

"Nooo, no way," she said, surprised. She didn't know him well, but she knew he loved her best friend.

"Yes ma'am, I caught her over there yesterday and today I

went by there and I let him convince me that what I saw yesterday was not true and after we made love I found that hoe's panties in the sheets."

"Damn, what did he say?"

"Said some shit about her putting them there on purpose, like I'm a damn fool."

"Well Lei that is something to consider. I mean, Ray is a good guy."

"Come on now Renee, if your husband told you that would you believe him?"

"Yeah, you're right. It's just hard to believe. I mean, Ray is romantic, kind and he is so good to you - to just up and cheat."

"I know that is why I don't think it's his first time; hell, who knows how many of them hoes he has been with?"

"Lei, I don't believe that. As big as them tricks' mouths are, one of them would have been put him on Front Street," Renee said and it made sense. Rayshon never hesitated to make it known to any of his female clients that he was with her.

"Yeah maybe so, but I don't know what to do now."

"Just please tell me you're not considering going back to Devon?"

"Are you crazy? I'm hurt, but I am not stupid."

"I'm just saying Lei, when you are emotional and going through is when you are so weak when it comes to Devon," she said, speaking the facts.

"No, Devon and I are history. We are done and I wouldn't take him back if a million Rays cheated on me," she said and laughed a little. Devon had done her in and made too, too many fake ass promises and to go back to him was like going back to hell. He lied so much and put her down too many times and she wasn't going to allow him another opportunity to hurt her, no matter how much he thinks he's changed. Devon was not an option, so Renee had nothing to fear.

She finished talking to Renee and managed to make it through a few moments without crying. Ray tried calling so many times until she powered off her phone and unplugged her house phone. Every time she was tempted to answer, the image of Katrina in that towel entered her mind and she didn't give in. She felt like a fool for giving in to him earlier and wished she didn't have to go over and get the rest of her stuff.

She stood in the mirror, looked at herself and wondered why he felt it necessary to mess around with his ex.? Was it the way she looked, or because she was not as sexy and beautiful as Katrina was? She looked at her image and compared herself to Katrina and she thought she was a Freddy Jackson to Katrina being a Janet Jackson. That's why you want her over me, is what she said as the tears began to form again. Just like Devon wanted Michelle over me. Maybe if I didn't have these rolls here or if my thighs were slimmer or my breast were perky is what she thought as she pulled, stretched and moved her skin. She hated her body and Ray didn't make her feel any better by cheating on her with Miss America.

She wiped the tears and decided she'd get out of the mirror. She blew out some air and went down to see her baby. She was disappointed when Devon told her that Deja was already sleeping.

"Well you don't have to hang around Devon. I'm good," she said.

"Lei, I know your man did something to hurt you and you can talk to me. I don't like seeing you like this," he said, trying to be there for her.

"Oh really? I guess you don't recall me being like this when you had me like this? You don't remember me being like this over you? You can't recall when you had me like this day in and out, but when Ray has me like this, you hate it."

"Leila, you know what I mean. I fucked up, yes and I didn't like seeing you like this then or now. You don't deserve to be sad and hurt or upset by me or any other man, okay? I am not happy about what I did to you or the bullshit I put you through."

"Devon please, okay? Worry about your issues and don't concern yourself with my issues with Ray. I am a lot stronger now, thanks to you and I am going to bounce back okay, so please spare me. You did a number on me too, remember?" she said and went into the kitchen to get a drink and he followed her.

"I know I did a number on you and our relationship and I am paying for it every day. Each night that I can't come home to you or have you the way I want to have you Leila, I am paying for it. I know I can't dog your man out for whatever it is he has done, but I do care about you and your happiness, so don't think for one moment that I wouldn't be concerned or worried about you. I told you months ago that I never want to see you cry or hurt again. And seeing you like this right now is killing me Leila, because I can't make you feel better," he said and Leila stood there. She didn't have nothing to say to Devon because deep down she was still angry with him for their failed marriage.

"Excuse me Devon," she said, grabbed her glass and went upstairs. His kind words penetrated her heart and she couldn't stand him trying to be so good when he used to be so bad. She sat on the ottoman and after two large swallows of her wine, she felt like screaming. Why was her life going in so many directions, filled with so many emotions? Devon was cruel and Ray came along and removed the dark clouds. Now Ray was the storm and Devon was trying to be her sunshine. She polished off the rest of her drink and climbed in bed. A couple hours later, Devon came in and she wished he would just go home and leave her alone.

"Lei," he whispered.

"Yeah," she replied.

"Can I come in?" he asked and she rolled her eyes.

"Sure," she said, letting him in because she knew he wasn't going to leave her alone. He climbed in bed with her and she kept her back to him. They were silent at first, but she was sniffling.

"What did he do to you sweetheart?" Devon asked again.

"Why, Devon? Why doesn't anyone want me?" she asked and he was shocked because all he had been doing the past few months was try to come back, so what did she mean?

"Lei, that's crazy," he replied.

"No, it's not crazy Devon. Am I just that hideous and disgusting that I can't keep a man interested? As soon as the perfect size five appears, I'm forgotten."

"No, that's not true Leila. That's nonsense. I want you," he said.

"You want me now, but when you had me, Devon, you didn't want me."

"Leila, I was a fool. I messed up, but trust me, my love, you are incredibly beautiful. When I first laid eyes on you, I couldn't get you outta my mind. I couldn't think of another woman. I had to have you Leila. Don't you remember when we were in college, how I followed you everywhere and begged you to go out with me a million times and when you finally said yes I think I did the running man all the way back to my dorms? You are so smart, brave and strong and good and if I hadda been the man that I was supposed to have been and cherished you like a real man, I would be looking at your beautiful face every morning.

"I was so busy focusing on images and too busy looking at the type of women the other executives had on their arms 'til I forgot about how beautiful the woman was I already had. I got lost in that bullshit Lei and I'm so sorry babe for what I put you through and what you are going through now. Whomever this cat is choosing to be with over you has nothing to do with the way you look okay, so get that out of your mind. You are so beautiful Leila, you are. I know I may have messed up your head with the insults and all the garbage I said to you about your weight, but I was wrong," he said sincerely.

"I know Devon and I know you are sorry. I just don't know why every time I fall in love I end up losing my man to another woman," she cried.

"You're not losing Lei. We are the ones who lost. If your relationship ended with this Ray guy over him and another woman, it has nothing to do with your looks and I betcha any amount of money he is going to realize choosing another over you was the biggest mistake of his life," he said and Leila knew that he was referring to himself as well. She closed her eyes and let Devon hold her and comfort her. It felt nice to be in his arms, but she didn't confuse what was going on and she was happy at that moment to have him as a friend.

XXX

Ray was going out of his mind. He was so mad at Katrina; he knew he'd strangle her to death if he saw her again. How in the world was he going to get Leila back, he wondered, after finding panties, an earring and make-up on his sheets? Katrina really fucked him for sure, he thought as he paced the floor. The towel scene was the work of an evil bitch and he couldn't believe that after all he has done to help her she'd obliterate his relationship with his woman. He didn't want to cry, but he broke down after his one hundredth attempts to call Leila.

For the first time since he started his own business, he was on the phone canceling appointments because he knew he'd be no good the next day. He just couldn't function because the fear of him never getting her back was sitting on his lap. He called her, texted her and e-mailed her and she didn't reply. He paced, cried, yelled and threw things across the room. After he boxed his bag and ran four miles on the treadmill, he was still too wired to shut his eyes. He called Leila repeatedly until he finally grabbed his keys to go to her house.

His heart dropped into the pit of his stomach when he saw Devon's car in her driveway. "Son of a bitch!" he yelled angrily and let the tears fall. Why would she run back to him? Why would she tell him that she didn't want Devon and as soon as they break up he was right back with her? He contemplated ringing the doorbell anyway, but he knew that that may have made things worse so he just sat there for hours. He stayed until after three and he knew then that Devon was there for the night.

He, at that moment, hated everyone - himself for allowing Katrina to come in and Katrina for being such an evil bitch and Leila for running back to Devon and Devon for being there for her. He clenched the steering wheel and forced himself to crank the engine and drive back to his loft. He asked God to put Katrina on the road so he could just run her ass over, but he knew that wasn't going to happen. He just cried and drove home, feeling like he had just been in a plane crash.

By the time he turned the key to his loft, he was in horrible shape. He was glad that his clients understood that he had to cancel because he would have not made it through that Friday under no circumstances without having Leila back. He knew he'd be in no shape to move the next morning.

It was five a.m. and it was a knock on the door. Ray jumped and looked at the clock. He heard the knocking again and he thought about Leila. He dashed to the door and was surprised to see Christa.

"Hey," she said, waiting for him to let her in.

"Christa," he said, surprised to see her.

"Aren't you going to let me in?" she asked and he was still confused.

"You didn't get my message?" he asked, remembering he left the message with her roommate.

"What message?"

"About me canceling our appointment today? I talked to your roommate. When I called your phone, she said you were in the shower."

"Oh well by the time I was out, my roommate was gone, so I didn't get the message," she said, looking at him as if to say *I still want my session.*

"Listen, come on in and I'm sorry, but I am going to need a minute," he said and let her come in.

"That's fine. I don't have much to do today," she said, coming in and this time she sat on the sofa. She looked around and wondered why Ray's loft looked a mess. That was not usual. He came out about twenty minutes later and she knew things were not right. "Ray, what's wrong? I've never seen you this unprofessional before and your place is crazy, man," she said, looking around.

"Christa, this is not a good time, okay?" he said and sat down on the chair. As masculine and strong as he was, his eyes burned with tears.

"Ray, what happened? What's going on?" she asked, concerned. He would have never talked to Christa about his personal life before, but he needed to.

"We broke up..., Leila and I broke up," he said, blinking back the tears.

"What? Why...? What happened?"

"The pretty girl on the couch is what happened."

"What did she do?"

"Well let's just say she fucked me," he said, letting the tears fall.

"Ray man, I'm sorry. I can't imagine what she could have done to break up your relationship with Leila. I mean, she slept on your sofa. That's not grounds for a break up in my opinion."

"Well Christa, she did a little more than that," he said, wiping his face.

"What, you didn't mess with her, did you Ray?"

"Hell no, I love Leila and you of all people know that."

"I do Ray, but it doesn't make sense to me," she said, confused.

"Well this is what went down," he said, telling Christa the

entire story. By the end, she was sitting there with her hand over her mouth. She had done some trifling things in her life too, but Katrina's story topped all of hers.

"My God Ray, I'm sorry. That is fucked up."

"Yep, but I guess I got what I deserved," he said with his head down.

"No, that is not true. You of all brothers are a good man. I know that you love Leila and I don't believe for one second that you would do that to her. I'm so sorry man," she said, being a friend.

"Thanks," he said and got up. He put on a pot of coffee and he and Christa ended up talking until after ten that morning. He felt a little better talking to her, but he had to remind her about her gossiping. "Now Christa, I know you know a lot of my clients, but please, if you can, don't go telling my business please. I talked to you this morning, not you and your girlfriends."

"Ray you're right? I respect you and I promise I will not share our conversation with anyone," she said and he believed her. She got up and he walked her to the door.

"Thanks for listening," he told her.

"Anytime and Ray, again I am sorry about you and Leila. I saw how happy you were to be with her," she said and he smiled.

"I just hope I can get her back."

"All things happen for a reason Ray and she loves you. If you guys are meant to be, no matter how much time goes by you will be together."

"Yeah," he said and nodded.

"If you need anything, let me know," she said and gave him a warm smile. "I'll see you Monday," she said and headed down the hall. He closed the door and wondered how he was going to spend the rest of his day with no Leila.

Now You Wanna Come Back

XXXI

"No, no, no, this can't be," Leila said, looking at the pregnancy results on the home kit she picked up from Walgreen's. She was in denial for two months and she finally couldn't ignore her missed periods. She was carrying Ray's child and she wondered how she was going to raise two kids by herself because she definitely didn't want to be with either of their fathers. Although she was still in love with Ray, she decided she wasn't going back. "Dear God no," she cried and sat on the tiled floor in her bathroom. She knew it happened on the last day they were together.

She knew it was Ray's because she and Devon were on a friendship level and they hadn't had sex at all. "Shit, shit, shit," she screamed and put her face in her hands and sobbed. She sat there for what seemed like hours until her phone snapped her back to reality. It was Devon, so she picked up.

"Hey beautiful," he chimed.

"Hey," she said, not as upbeat as he was.

"What's wrong?" he asked.

"Nothing, what's up?"

"Do you want me to get DJ or what? I need to know before I head home."

"Yes please. I was a little sick today, so I'm at the house and not at the store," she said.

"Again Lei, you may want to see a doctor," he suggested.

"I am tomorrow," she said, although she knew what the problem was.

"Okay, well I'll get DJ and I'll keep her tonight. We will see you tomorrow. Feel better," he said and they hung up. She and he were doing so well and she knew he'd be willing to give her a divorce come court time and she was happy about that. She went downstairs and fixed herself a sandwich and before she could finish eating it, she was throwing up again. "Damn you Ray, why did I let you do this to me?" she yelled and went for the crackers.

She debated when and how she would tell him. She wondered would he even believe her. She finished downstairs and went into the bathroom to take a shower. She looked at the test again and she didn't cringe. She thought back to her pregnancy with Deja and how happy she was and she wanted to be happy with her second baby too, so she smiled. "I hope you are a boy, because if you are, you'll be the last one to occupy this space," she said, touching her tummy.

She actually felt better by the time she got into bed. The next day she went to the doctor and he confirmed that she was pregnant and due in August. She got to the store that afternoon and she didn't want to tell her secret, but she just had to tell Renee.

"Well Renee, Deja's going to be a big sister," she said, smiling.

"What?" she asked shocked. "You're pregnant?"

"Yep, Dr. Bryce confirmed it this morning. That's why I've been sick every other day.

"Wow, my God. How in the hell did you get pregnant? Well I know how, but I thought you said you and Devon weren't sleeping together?"

"We're not; Ray's the father," she said, being honest.

"What? How?" she asked.

"Well the last day we were together. That was the magical day we didn't use any protection," she said, looking away.

"So when are you going to tell him?

"Huh?" she said, as if she forgot she was going to have to tell him.

"When are you going to tell Ray?" she asked again and Leila had no idea. She knew she had to tell him, but she didn't know when. She went back and forth in her mind with how and when. Then, two months later, she still hadn't told him. She was almost five months and showing when the judge saw her and Devon again. When she told the judge that Devon was not the father, he granted her divorce quickly. Devon wasn't too happy because he was still trying to work it out, even though he knew he wasn't her baby's father.

By the time she was seven months along, she still had not talked to Ray. She tried every day to tell him but didn't know how. She thought about e-mailing him, writing him a letter, or even sending him a text message, but none of those options would have been right and she was so terrified to face him. No matter how she tried, the days went by and she hadn't told him. She was at the store one afternoon and almost fainted when Christa walked in.

"Leila, is that you?" Christa asked having no idea Leila owned that bookstore.

"Yes Christa, it's me. How are you?" she asked nervously. She was seven and a half months and larger than life.

"I've been good. How have you been?" she asked nicely and Leila thought that was odd because Christa was never that nice or courteous.

"Okay and pregnant, as you can see," she said, holding her tummy.

"Oh, yes, I can definitely see that. How far along are you?"

"Seven and a half months," she said, wishing she would have

lied. She was sure they all knew when she and Ray broke up.

"Well I know you haven't spoken to Ray and I know he has no idea that you are carrying his child," Christa said bluntly, being the Christa that Leila remembered.

"What makes you think its Ray's child?" she asked with a little attitude. Who did Christa think she was?

"Well Leila, thinking back, it was 'bout seven months ago when you guys split and if Ray would have known, he'd be bragging about his first child every day," she said and Leila was speechless. "You really should tell him Leila. He is a good guy," she said, defending the cheating dog, Leila thought to herself.

"So he's fucking you now?" Leila asked, wondering why she was defending him.

"Wow Leila, I'd never expect to hear something like that from you, but the answer is no. Ray has been my personal trainer for years and he has always been professional with not only me, but with all of us. The thing is, when you guys broke up, he was devastated behind it and it took him a long time to get back to normal. He loved you and I know he'd be there for his child and you not telling him is wrong."

"Do you know what he did to me Christa? He lied to me and I tried to tell him…, I have."

"Well Leila, you can believe me or not believe me, but the morning that you say he lied to you was my Wednesday appointment and I was there that Wednesday at five a.m. and when I got there that chick was on the sofa under a beige comforter. That is where she was when I got there and when I left. On my way out, I saw Patricia parking her car. Now, if they did it and she got up to get dressed and got on the sofa hey, I can't say, but I doubt that he slept with her and I do believe that chick crazy.

"Two other clients that saw him that day can vouch that she was rude and nasty. Ray is a good man and he needs to know Leila. Even if you don't want him back, you need to tell him," Christa said and she was not sure if she could trust her.

"So, you are sure she was on the sofa?"

"Yes ma'am, fully dressed and even had on a pair of boots, if I remember correctly, they were some red boots because her feet were not covered," she said and it made sense. Who would have sex, get up, get dressed and go to the sofa? If Ray wanted to hide her, he would have made her stay in the room so none of his clients could see her. "I can understand how you felt, Leila, but this is a baby," she said and she was right.

"You're right, Christa, okay? I know I have to tell him, so please don't tell him, let me," she begged.

"Not a problem, just don't wait too long because it looks like you are about to pop," she joked and they laughed.

"I know, right?" she said.

"Well let me assure you. I go to Ray three to four times a week and I have not seen that girl at all, so he is not with her," she said and Leila was happy to hear that.

"I believe you and I'm going to tell him."

"Alright, now show me where the romance novels are because I need a good one."

"Okay, follow me," she said and helped Christa get what she needed. Christa used to be the last bitch she would trust, but that day she was a better Christa and Leila thanked God for sending her someone to help her do the right thing.

XXXII

"I know you always tell me to mind my business Ray, but over the past few months we have been cool and I consider you and me to be friends," Christa told him the next morning. She didn't know if he had talked to Leila yet, but she felt it was only right to tell him that she saw her and that she was pregnant.

"Okay now Christa, you know I don't like gossip," he said, helping her with her sit-ups.

"I know, Ray and normally I'd keep my mouth shut, but I saw Leila yesterday."

"Don't…, I don't want to hear anything about that woman, okay? I told you months ago to never mention her name to me again," he said, not wanting to revive any memories of her. He was finally able to make it through an entire day without shedding a few tears.

"Ray, this is important and I know you don't wanna hear about her or talk about her, but you really should go by the store to see her," she said, not wanting to just spill the beans.

"No, I shouldn't and leave it alone, Christa."

"Ray come on, it's been, what - over seven months and I

know you are curious to know how she is."

"No, I'm not," he snapped and got up. "Damn Christa, why did you have to mention that woman's name?"

"You still love her, don't you? I know you do," she said, pausing from her workout. She was not the same Christa she was months ago. She and Ray had a better relationship and he shared his feelings with her a lot after the break up, so that's why she knew he needed to know.

"Yes, as much as I hate to admit it I do," he said and rubbed his head.

"Look, I'm not telling you what to do, but I really think you ought to go and see her."

"Did she ask about me?"

"Yeah, she did and I know she still loves you. I know you guys miss each other," she said, going for a towel.

"That may be true, but Leila may not wanna see me."

"Well it wouldn't hurt to try," she said, nudging his arm. They finished their workout and all he thought about for the rest of the day was Leila and how nice it would be to see her. He didn't know how smooth it would go, but he thought it would be good. When he got to the store, her truck was not outside and he was a bit disappointed. He sat in his truck for a few moments and waited and then his cell phone rang. To his surprise, it was Leila. After all, of that time, he still didn't delete her number from his contacts and he almost dropped the phone trying to answer it.

"Hello," he said nervously and his palms began to sweat.

"Hey, is this a bad time?"

"No..., no your timing is perfect."

"Listen Ray, I know it's been a long time since we have spoken and I know you may have moved on and are probably not interested in talking to me, but I have to talk to you."

"I mean, I can't believe you're on the other end of this phone. I would love to see you and talk to you. Just say when and where," he said eagerly. She didn't want to see him, but she knew she had to tell him about the baby, especially before he heard it from someone else. She knew if Christa ran and told him it may be a bad thing because Christa didn't seem to like her very much. She was so surprised how nice Christa was to her the day before, she had to blink twice after she walked out of her store because Christa didn't come across as the *"Tin Woman"* she knew from before; she actually acted as if she had a heart.

"Well tonight is good. I'm available and I would like to see you again," he said, not pretending. He would have taken any opportunity to see her or be around her and he hoped they could work it out.

"Tonight? I was thinking this weekend or you know, next week sometime," she said, knowing that she didn't need to push this out any further. She was already seven and a half months and she knew he may strangle her when he found out that she had kept her pregnancy from him.

"Wow, next week huh?" he said, disappointed.

"Listen Ray, it's been awhile and what I have to talk to you about is very important and I'm so scared to even face you right now," she said, preparing him for her secret.

"There is nothing you can't tell me and I don't care how long it's been, okay? I just wanna see you, so whatever it is, it's okay. I am the one who caused us to break up and I'm so sorry for allowing Katrina to come in and mess up our good thing. Baby I swear, even if we never get back together, I did not touch that woman. When I was with you, I was with you," he said and she was quiet. The tears started to burn her eyes and if it had not been for Christa telling her what she saw that morning, she still would have not called him. "Leila, are you there?" he asked.

"Yes, I'm here," she said softly.

"So, how about it? Can I see you tonight?" he asked and her

stomach got queasy and his son started to kick as if to say, "Go on mom, see him and tell him about me."

"Okay," she said, not believing she agreed.

"So, can I come by or do you wanna come by my place?"

"Your place is fine. I can be there in maybe two hours. I gotta get Deja to Devon and then I can come by."

"Wow, how is Deja? I miss her so much. She was like my little girl too, you know?" he said and she smiled. He didn't have to pretend anymore because he had a son on the way.

"Yeah, I know and she is a big girl now. Hopefully, you will see her soon."

"Yeah, I hope so too," he said and they were quiet. She was smiling and so was he.

"Listen Ray, when you see me I may look a little different. You know I haven't been working out or eating right since you and I broke up," she said, referring to her huge tummy and plump face. She was still beautiful and to be pregnant, she hadn't gained too much weight, but she sure looked very pregnant.

"I don't care about any of that Leila, because you've always been beautiful. I just wanna see you, all of you - no matter how big, how small, I just wanna see you," he said and Leila was more touched. Rayshon always made her feel beautiful from day one, something Devon stopped doing when she put on the pounds.

"So, I'll see you in a little while," she said, pulling into the guest-parking stall at Devon's condominium.

"Okay, I'll see you," he said and they hung up. She called Devon and he came down to get Deja because she was sleeping and Leila could not carry her anymore. She was a little over two and too heavy for a pregnant woman to be carrying. Leila pulled out and hurried home to shower and get prettied up. Bad enough she was twenty-five pounds heavier, she couldn't show up looking like a clown. She was pregnant and glowing. She put on one of her cutest maternity outfits and put on some make up. Her hair was thick and shiny, thanks to her pregnancy and she was so happy that she had gone to the salon that afternoon. She stood in the mirror and convinced herself that she could go through with it and headed out the door.

When she arrived, she sat in the truck, took a few deep breaths and opened the door. She opened the entry door to his building and contemplated on getting back in her truck to go home. "You can do this, you can do this," she said to herself and she heard a door open and she froze. It was one of Ray's neighbors and as soon as they cleared the hall, she headed for the elevator before she lost her nerve. She tapped on the door a few times and she turned her back when she heard him unlocking the dead bolt. She was so nervous, she thought she'd pass out, but as soon as she heard his voice, she knew she was doing the right thing.

XXXIII

"Hey," he said and she turned slowly. "Come on...," he said and he looked at her stomach.

"I told you I looked different," she said, trying to crack a joke and he didn't laugh or smile. He was so disappointed to see her stomach because he thought she and Devon were back together and there was no chance for them to work it out.

"Wow Leila, you are beautiful," he said, looking at her perfect glowing complexion.

"May I come in?" she asked because she was still standing in the hall.

"Sure, sure...," he said, moving out of her way and letting her come inside. He shut the door and offered her a seat. "Wow Leila, you've changed for sure."

"Yeah, I have and I see you are still fine and fit as ever," she said, smiling at the built and sexy ass man that she no longer had.

"Yeah, well I just focus on work and you know, going on with my life - and I see you've definitely gone on with your life. How far are you? I know Devon is happy."

"Well I am about 7½ months and Devon wasn't happy at first, but now he is okay, I guess. He helps me a lot and we are finally divorced," she said, smiling. "The judge got wind of me carrying another's man child and he finally gave me the divorce," she said, making it known that Devon was not her child's father and they were no longer married.

"Wow, not Devon, huh?" he asked, sitting on the arm of the sofa and even more disappointed.

"No," she said and swallowed hard and looked away. "Devon isn't the father of my baby," she said and Ray was about to pass out. They had broken up about seven and a half months ago and she went out, got another man that fast and got pregnant. He was outdone.

"Hold on, give me a minute," he said, getting up and going into the kitchen. He grabbed a glass and hit a shot of rum to calm himself. "Do you want anything?" he asked before he went back into the living room.

"No, I'm good," she said. "Ray listen, this is so hard for me and I have wanted to call you so many times, but I was so afraid."

"It's cool. You have a new life, a new man and I can understand," he said, not allowing her to finish.

"Huh?" she asked, looking at him strange.

"Your baby, I'm sure you and the father are happy," he said and she understood what he thought.

"Oh, you think I am with someone?" she asked and he just looked at her. "Ray, I'm not with anyone. I have not been with anyone since we broke up," she said and he was confused. How was she pregnant if she hadn't been with anyone else?

"Excuse me?" he said, leaning forward.

"Ray, I am carrying your son," she said and he hopped off the couch.

"No fucking way," he yelled, walking back toward the kitchen. He grabbed the rum and his glass, took another shot and decided to bring the bottle and glass into the living room with him.

"Ray, I'm so sorry; I didn't want to tell you like this."

"Leila, how you gon' come up in here and tell me this shit almost eight months later?" he yelled and slammed the rum down on the coffee table and it made her jump. He realized he was overreacting, so he brought it down a notch. "Listen Leila, baby, I'm sorry. I didn't mean to yell," he said, gaining his composure. "I mean this is just…," he tried to say and took another shot. He was overwhelmed and shocked and he knew he had to lay off the rum, but she just dropped a bomb in his lap.

"I know, Ray and I was just as surprised as you are now."

"Leila, you could have told me. I mean, I would have been there for you," he said honestly. "I mean, look at you," he said, getting up, moving closer to her. "Can I?" he asked, wanting to touch her stomach.

"Yes," she said, placing his hand on the spot where her baby was kicking.

"Oh my God Leila. This is real. I can feel him moving."

"Yeah, he has been doing summersaults ever since we spoke on the phone earlier."

"Oh Leila, it's a boy? How long have you've known he was a boy?"

"Since maybe sixteen weeks," she said and Ray just went on his knees and rubbed her stomach like it was impossible for her to be pregnant with his baby.

"Why didn't you tell me baby? I can't understand why you wouldn't tell me," he asked, looking her in the eye. His eyes welled and he wanted to hug her and strangle her at the same time.

"I don't know Ray. I was so scared and nervous and I knew if I would have been around you and wasn't over you it would have been more difficult for me. I was heartbroken, confused and one day turned into another day and then another and then yesterday. Christa came into the store and we talked and I begged her to allow me the opportunity to tell you myself," she said and he was angry.

"So, if you had not saw Christa yesterday, you would not have told me?" he asked, turning away from her.

"Ray, I don't know when, but I know I would have told you," she said nervously.

"When, Leila? After my son was born?" he asked angrily.

"You know what Ray? You are so right and the conversation we are having right now is the reason why the days continued to go by and I couldn't tell you, because no matter when I told you, I know you would have reacted this same way and I was afraid of that," she said, with watery eyes.

"No Leila, you can't say what I would have done because you didn't give me a choice," he said, getting up and walking over to the window.

"Okay Ray. Now you know, so I'll go," she said, struggling to get out of the low chair and he rushed over to her.

"No Leila, wait okay? I don't want you to go, okay? Sit down and let me get you some water," he said and she settled back down in the chair. He brought her a bottle of water and she opened it and took a few swallows. They sat there quiet for a while, not even looking at each other. Leila rubbed her stomach because her baby was on ten that evening and he wasn't settling down. She was frowning because he was kicking pretty hard. "Are you okay?" he asked, getting up, moving closer to her.

"Yes, I'm okay. He is just doing a dance on me right now and I don't know why he is this excited tonight."

"Maybe it's because he is here in the place where he was conceived," he said, kneeling down in front of her again. He began rubbing her stomach again and Leila liked him touching her and touching her swollen belly. She took deep breaths and her body gave her signs of how much she missed Ray because she wanted him to kiss her and rub her in other places. "Do you mind?" he asked, wanting to lift her shirt.

"No," she said and he lifted her shirt and looked at her strangely when he saw the maternity elastic over her stomach. "They are maternity pants, Ray," she said, laughing.

"Oh, I've never seen a pair of pants like this," he said and she pushed the elastic down, exposing her bare belly. It was smooth and the dark line up the middle of her belly was the true sign of a pregnant woman. "Wow," he said, rubbing his hands across her smooth stomach.

"I know it's huge," she said.

"Yes it is, but it is beautiful," he said, putting his face close to her. He couldn't help himself and he kissed her stomach softly and she let him.

"You know, I never stopped thinking about you for one day," she told him.

"How could you? Every time you look down there's a round reminder of me," he said and they laughed. It tickled Ray to see how her stomach jumped as she laughed. "I never stopped thinking of you one minute Leila and I do wish you hadda told me earlier about the baby, but I'm happy that you told me now."

"I am too and I'm so relieved to have finally gotten that out. I feel like I dropped one hundred pounds," she said.

"Well it looked like you picked up about eighty," he joked, holding her stomach.

"Ha, ha," she said.

"You know I'm just joking," he said, getting up and reaching for her hand.

"What?" she said, giving him her hand.

"Come on, I want you to sit with me on the sofa," he said and they moved over to the couch. She sat down and he sat at the opposite end, took one of her feet and removed her shoe. A foot massage was a great idea and she didn't resist his gesture.

"So, are you seeing anyone?" she asked, afraid to hear his response.

"Nope, I'm still a single man."

"Why is that?"

"Well I fell in love with this one woman that dropped me cold when she thought I cheated on her and I just could never seem to get over her, so I'm still single. Are you seeing anyone?" he asked, knowing she wasn't. She had just told him she hadn't been with anyone since their break up.

"Please man, look at me. I look like a root beer float. I can't get a man walking around pregnant and swollen."

"Really? I find that hard to believe."

"Come on Ray, be serious."

"No, I am serious. You are radiant."

"Well when most men see a pregnant woman, they are not thinking she's available."

"True," he said and continued to rub her foot. They were quiet for a moment and he reached for her other foot. "So, if I asked you out, would you be willing to go out with me?" he asked and she smiled

"Well let's see, I'll have to check my schedule," she said jokingly.

"Oh, it's like that, huh?"

"Nah, I'm kidding. How about you go out with me, let's say tomorrow around three?" she asked.

"Let me see, tomorrow at three I have Mia and at four Jada. How about tomorrow evening?"

"Well I don't mind tomorrow evening, but tomorrow I have a doctor's appointment. I thought you'd like to come along and hear the baby's heartbeat and check out his photo shoot."

"Photo shoot?" he asked puzzled.

"His ultrasound. I have been having a slight rise with my blood pressure and the doctor just wants to take a look to make sure he is fine," she said, not wanting to make a big deal.

"Slightly? How slight?" he asked seriously.

"Don't worry Ray, I'm fine," she tried to convince him.

"Look Leila, your health is a very serious thing and tomorrow, even though I know you are 7½ months, you and I are going for a 30 minute walk and I'm not taking no for an answer. We can't have your blood pressure high."

"Come on Ray, I get out of breath so easily now. I can't go for a walk," she said, trying to get out of it.

"It's okay; we will walk a pregnant pace. I will not hurt you Leila. I love you and I want you healthy," he said tenderly and she smiled. He said that to her tons of times when they were together. He would always say, *'I don't want you skinny, Leila; I just want you healthy.'*

"Okay Ray, I hear you, but what about your appointments?"

"Don't worry about that; just let me take care of that and I will also take care of you and the baby," he said and Leila was relieved that he didn't kick her out after telling him that he was the father.

"Ray I love you too and you just don't know how much I've missed you and how many times I wanted to just call or come by. I was so lonely and sad without you."

"Leila, we can work our thing out if you want to. We have a baby coming and the offer still stands," he said, talking about the proposal.

"You still wanna marry me?" she asked, surprised.

"Yes, I still wanna marry you. Do you wanna marry me?" he asked and she was speechless.

"Yes, Ray I do," she said, nodding up and down.

"Okay," he said and smiled at her.

"So, where do we go from here?"

"Well we can go into the bedroom and do some making up, or we can stay out here and watch TV and talk."

"Option A sounds good," she said and he laughed.

"I figured it would," he said, getting up and helping her up. She hadn't done it since the last time they did it and with all that belly in the way things felt strange at first, but like riding a bike, it came back to them quickly. They were exhausted when they were done and they collapsed on top of the covers. "I see pregnant stuff is good stuff," he joked.

"What?" she asked surprised at what he said.

"You know, guys say pregnant stuff is the best stuff."

"Well my stuff has always been good," she said.

"No doubt baby, it has. It was just extra good tonight. And, I don't know if it has to do with the pregnancy, but damn, I want some more," he said.

"Already?" she asked.

"Yes, ma'am. Need I remind you I haven't had you in almost eight months?"

"Well I haven't had you either."

"And I am gonna make sure we never have to say those words again."

"You promise?"

"I promise baby."

XXXIV

The next morning the sound of music woke Leila up. That was a sound she missed and she smiled to be back in his bed. She eased out of bed, went into the bathroom and sat on the toilet for a few moments after she was done. She looked around the bathroom and it was clean as a whistle, like she remembered it being. She went to the vanity to wash her hands and face and realized her toothbrush was still on the other sink that she used to use. She wondered if it had been there since the break up or if he pulled it out when he knew she was coming by. After they broke up, she never went back to get any of her things, so she went to her drawer and was floored that her things were still in there.

She went through her stuff and wondered if she could fit any one of the bras because she knew the panties were not going to fit. She showered and put on a pair of her old thongs and it sat underneath her stomach. She couldn't fit any of the bras, so she had to put the one she had back on. She went through Ray's walk-in closet and found an oversized Chicago Bears jersey and put it on. She went and got her purse from the living room to call Renee and even though her picture was not on the coffee table, there were a couple of her and Deja on his mantle and bookshelves.

She walked over to them and could see the difference in her face from when she lost a few pounds versus her pregnant face. To think, after all those months and her being afraid to tell him were wasted and he still wanted her back. "You are too good to be true," she said, thinking about Ray out loud. She wondered where he put her baby's playpen and toys because they were going to come in handy for the new baby.

She sat on the sofa, called Renee and brought her up to date on what was going on. She was so elated she couldn't talk without a huge smile on her face. When she was done, she headed for the kitchen and she decided to eat some fruit and a toasted bagel. She opened the fridge and was shocked to see strawberry creamed cheese, the stuff Ray vowed was no good for her. "Um huh, got you hooked on the creamed cheese too," she said and smiled again. When she sat on the stool, she heard the music stop and she knew Ray's session was coming to an end.

She couldn't remember who would be there that Wednesday from seven 'til eight, but she immediately recognized her face when she came down.

"Wow Leila, what a surprise. How are you?" she asked with a warm smile and Leila stood.

"I'm good, nice to see you again," she said, trying to remember her name. She was definitely a regular, but her name was hard for Leila to remember.

"Oh and you are having a baby. Ray didn't tell me you guys were back together and he certainly didn't tell me about your little bundle," she said as if she knew the baby wasn't Ray's.

"Yes, well our son will be arriving soon," Leila said, correcting her. He was not her bundle; he was their bundle.

"Ray's going to be a dad? Get out, no way," she said and Leila wondered if that meant, *"Stop yo' lying, that ain't his baby."*

"Yes Rayshon, is going to be a daddy," she said and he came down the steps.

"Good morning. How did you sleep?" he asked Leila and kissed her on the forehead.

"Amazing, I didn't realize how much I missed that bed," she said and then realized Patricia was still standing there. Patricia, yeah that's her name, she suddenly remembered.

"Well congratulations to you both," she said, getting ready to make her exit.

"Thank you Patricia," Leila said.

"Yeah, thanks and I'll see you on Saturday," Ray said, shutting the door behind her. "Well I have two more clients and then I'm all yours," he said, walking over to Leila.

"Ray it's eight in the morning, how did you manage that?"

"I rescheduled my entire afternoon appointments," he said and she wondered how he did that?

"All of them? Impossible," she said in disbelief. Ray was a busy man and was blessed to stay booked and kept back-to-back appointments.

"Well my people are cool and once I told them that I had to go with you for an ultrasound they said no problem," he said and Leila wondered how many non-believers she was about to get evil stares from, but who cared? "Now, I will be done in time for us to take a nice walk in the park and still make it to the doctor's on time," he said and the knock on the door took him away from their embrace.

"Duty calls," she said and smiled as he opened the door.

"Angela, come on in," he said and she walked in.

"Hey Ray, what's--," she was saying 'til she saw Leila.

"Hi Angela," Leila said with a warm smile.

"Leila my God, you're huge," she said without shame.

"I'm pregnant Angela," she said to the space ball. She was a size zero in the brains as well.

"Oh, I was gon' say," she said and Leila couldn't help but laugh. That poor girl was slower than Deja, Leila thought to herself.

"Babe, I'll see you shortly," he said and gave her a quick kiss and he and Angela went upstairs.

"Did she tell you that was yo kid?" she heard Angela whisper.

"It is my child Angela and for the hundredth time, my

personal business is not your business. Now, let's get started," Ray, said and Leila shook her head. She headed back to Ray's room and the phone rang. She thought back to the time when Katrina answered his phone and she decided not to do that. When his answering machine came on, it was her and Leila was tempted to snatch the phone off the hook, but she just listened to her.

"Rayshon, this is Kat again. I have left you thousands of messages. I have come by and left you notes. Like I said, the past is the past and it is time you forgive me and give me a chance. I'm sorry for lying to Leila and I don't know how to make you see I did it because I love you. Again, please call me. It's been more than seven months; you can't still be mad," she said and the machine beeped.

Leila looked down at the flashing light and it said twenty-one messages. She tried to resist, but she hit the play button. Of twenty-one messages, eighteen were from Katrina and the other three were telemarketers. She wondered if Ray even listened to any of the messages, but she figured he had not because they were all from the previous two days. She listened to Katrina breathe on the line 'til the machine cut her off. She listened to her cry and she listened to her angry *"I hate you"* ones. How could someone be hooked on someone for that long that refused to talk to them? She wondered, but it was obvious. Love was love. After all that time of her not talking to Ray, she still loved him and he still loved her, so she felt kind of sorry for Katrina, but also she felt like she got what she deserved.

One thing for sure, she was relieved that all of Katrina's attempts to talk to Ray were unanswered. Katrina did confirm that Rayshon made no efforts to see or talk to her since that incident. That made her feel like shit for treating Ray so horribly and not telling him about the baby. Her eyes welled when she thought about how much time she lost and how she couldn't go back. She regretted not telling him sooner. She touched her stomach and told her baby that she was sorry and that she made a mistake. She told him that from then on, she would never keep anything away from his father and she was going to do her part to make things perfect for all of them.

She wiped her eyes and she knew it may have been inappropriate, but she hit "Erase" and then erased all messages on his machine. She grabbed the remote, turned on the tube and waited for him to finish. After he saw his last client out, he went into his room and immediately started to undress.

"Katrina called," she said and hit the mute on the remote. He paused and looked at Leila.

"I don't talk to her Lei," he said, standing and hoping that this would not be another episode where she walked out on him.

"I know," she said and smiled and his heart started to beat again. "I just wanted to tell you something. Come here and sit," she said, sitting up in the bed. He sat down next to her. "I'm sorry for not believing you when you told me the truth. I'm sorry for walking out on you and for not telling you about the baby," she said and her eyes welled.

"Leila, baby -," he tried to say.

"No Rayshon, please hear me out. We've lost so much time and I should have trusted you Ray. I was so angry and I didn't believe that I was special enough for someone to love me. I had a horrible self-image about myself and it was easier to accept you wanted the sexy, petite, head turner Katrina over me. I didn't stop and see that looks had nothing to do with it. You gave back what Devon took from me. You treated me like I was more beautiful than Christa, Mia, Veronica and you never once acted like you were ashamed to be with the big girl, so I'm sorry for not having faith in what we had and let Katrina's ugly ass come between us.

"I listened to all of the messages that she left," she said, being honest. "And I deleted them too," she said and he looked over and the message light was no longer blinking. "Ray I trust you and I know that if no other man sees me to be beautiful, you do and I thank you for what you did for me back then and I thank you for holding onto me in your heart. You are my match and I see now that we are made for each other and I love you," she said and he touched her face.

"We are going to be okay. We have a new baby coming, we

have a promising future and I am going to see to it that nothing like that ever happens again. I am sorry too, for putting myself in a situation like I did with Kat and you had every right to feel like you felt because it did look pretty bad and I still to this day sometimes wonder what possessed that crazy ass girl to stuff her draws between my mattress and headboard," he said and they laughed. "But seriously Leila, it doesn't matter where we were then; all that matters is that I have you now," he said, pulling her close and kissing her passionately.

"You trying to get some?" she asked because he was tugging on the jersey.

"Oh yes and if you give me some, we don't have to do that walk," he said and stood to take off his sweats, revealing his beautiful erection.

"Oh, you don't have to ask me twice," she said, taking off the jersey. They did their thing again and Leila wondered how in the hell did she go seven and a half months without him.

XXXV

They finished and Ray still talked Leila into going for a walk in the park. They walked and held hands and Leila thought heaven had come down on earth for her that day. They sat on the bench for a little while because she still had a couple free moments before going to her appointment.

"Aw Leila, I'm so happy that we are here at this moment. This day..., I mean, it's beautiful, you are beautiful and this is just so perfect. I just hate I missed out on everything."

"Ray you didn't miss much. I mean, we still have weeks before he comes," she said, holding her belly.

"I did Leila. The first doctor's appointment, the five minute wait while the test processed, the cravings, the sickness," he said and she felt bad for cheating him out of that experience.

"Well babes, the cravings are still here, trust me. I wish I had a bagel with strawberry cream cheese right now and the sickness I have occasionally, but not often," she said, making faces. "And baby, if you want that stick test, we can run to Walgreen's, grab a test and you can watch it turn blue," she teased and they laughed.

"You're too much, you know that?" he said.

"No baby, you take the cake," she said.

"Well big momma, come on we better get going," he said, standing and reaching for her.

"Hey, what's with the big momma?"

"You are a big momma. All this belly and you are a momma," he said and she didn't think it was funny. "Come on babe, I'm joking. Don't get sensitive," he said, putting his arm around her neck.

"I'm not, but big momma is an insult."

"Is it? Well I didn't know that. What if I call you big hot momma because you were like fire at the house?" he said and she smiled.

"How about hot momma?" she said.

"I can do that," he said and they rode a couple blocks to the doctor's office. Ray sat there nervous as the nurse checked her vitals. Her blood pressure was normal and Ray knew it had to do with the sex and the nice walk in the park. He began to tremble when the doctor came in and got ready for the exam.

"Hello Leila, how are you feeling?" Dr. Bryce asked.

"I'm perfect," she responded, looking at Ray.

"I see and I'm happy to see that your pressure is normal and I am thrilled to see that you have a reason for the big smile on your face," he said, washing his hands. "You must be Rayshon Sr.?" Dr. Bryce asked and Ray wondered how he knew his name so well.

"Yes, I can say I am," Ray said nervously.

"Yeah, ever since day one, when we announced that Leila was carrying a boy, we all know him as Rayshon Jr.," Dr. Bryce said and Ray was so proud.

"Wow, I'm very anxious to meet my son too," Ray said and Leila held his hand.

"Well I'll let you guys listen to his heartbeat first and Leila, I know your pressure looks good today, but I'm going to do that ultrasound anyway just to be absolutely sure he is doing well," he said and pulled back her shirt. He got the gel from the warmer and squeezed it in a small spot and Ray got to hear his son's heartbeat for the first time. It sounded strange to him, he looked at Leila and the tears rolled down the side of her face. "Well his heartbeat sounds good and strong," Dr. Bryce said and the nurse came in to assist with the ultrasound.

By the time they turned on the lights, Ray was speechless. Dr. Bryce pointed out all of the baby's organs and genitals and Ray couldn't believe what he had just seen. He had never seen anything so amazing in his life. "Well Leila, it shouldn't be too much longer. Everything looks great and I want you to go home and take it easy and enjoy the next few weeks and August 19th we should see this little one in person," he said and Ray helped her from the table. "It was nice to meet you, Mr. Johnson and I know you guys working things out helped my patient's blood pressure, so take care of her and the baby for me," Dr. Bryce said and Ray shook his hand with a smile.

"Don't worry Dr. Bryce. I will take care of them," he said and they headed out. They got into Ray's truck and he was in a state of shock. It was like things couldn't be more perfect. "Leila baby, let's get married," he said and she looked at him.

"Huh?" she asked, surprised.

"Married baby. Let's just do it," he said seriously.

"Are you serious Ray?"

"Yes, let's get married right now. I don't want to go another day without you being my wife," he expressed and Leila was touched.

"Rayshon are you crazy? I mean, we live in separate houses and I mean baby, we just can't get married right now," she said, thinking he lost his mind.

"I don't care about us living in two separate houses Leila. That is small; we can work that out easily," he said, taking her hand. "Leila I want to marry you today. I don't want to wait."

"Baby, we got to get a license and we got to think about the house and the loft and Deja," she said, trying to be rational.

"Leila, do you love me?"

"Yes," she said softly.

"Do you want me?" he asked, pulling over.

"Of course I do," she said.

"Well there is not one reason for us not to do this. I love you Leila and I want my son to be born with his parents being married," he said and she could see in his eyes that he was serious.

"Okay then baby, let's get married," she said and he drove to the courthouse. They applied for the license and had to wait three days before they could actually get married. The following week, they were married and Leila's house and Ray's loft were on the market. They knew it would be tight, but they managed to find a house the second week and they put in a contract on it. Three mortgages would have been a stretch for them, but they were ready to do whatever it took to be under the same roof.

Leila was getting bigger and it was getting harder for her to move around, so she was at Ray's loft most of the time. She was eight and a half months and she still had not told Devon she and Ray were married. He knew the house was on the market, but he didn't know she was selling it because they were already married and Devon was at the house when he noticed Leila's left hand.

"Lei, let me see your finger," he asked.

"Huh?" she said, like she didn't hear him.

"Is that a band behind your engagement ring?" he asked and she didn't lie.

"Yes," she said and looked away.

"Lei, what's going on?"

"I'm married Devon. Ray and I got married three weeks ago," she said, confessing.

"What? You fucking got married behind my back?" he

snapped.

"No Devon. I got married and didn't tell you," she said.

"Why, Lei? Why would you not tell me?" he asked sadly.

"Devon I didn't want to hurt you okay? You were upset with me when you found out about how I was pregnant with Ray's baby and I thought you'd be upset with me getting married," she said.

"Listen Leila, we are divorced. You are damn near nine months pregnant and I know you love him and you didn't have to keep that from me," he said and she knew he was right.

"Devon you are right and I wanted to tell you, but I didn't know how, so there it is. I'm married and I'm happy," she said and tried to walk off, but he grabbed her hand.

"Lei, I'm glad you are happy. I am happy for you and you will always have a place in my heart and I will forever be here for you and Deja and this little stranger too, if you need me to be," he said and that made Leila feel good.

"Thanks Devon, thank you so much. I'm so happy to have you in my life as a friend. You have truly been a good friend to me and I thank you Devon, because I know it wasn't easy for either one of us to get to this point," she said and they hugged. Ray walked in the door and saw them embracing, but it didn't bother him.

"Hello Devon," he said, putting the bags on the island. "Baby, I got your favorite from the Chinese spot," he said and Devon took a deep breath and blew it out. He remembered picking up Leila's favorite Chinese, but he knew he was a horrible husband and now she was Ray's wife.

"Thanks baby," she said, looking in the bag. "I'm going to be right back. I gotta grab some things for DJ for Devon," she said and went up the steps, leaving them alone in the kitchen.

"Congratulations man," Devon said.

"Oh, Lei finally told you?" Ray asked, taking the food from the bags.

"Yeah, I had to ask, but she told me."

"Well I told her a hundred times to tell you, but you know Leila; she does things when she is ready," he commented.

"Yeah, I know her," he said and picked up Deja. "Listen Ray, we have two of the same women in common and I trust that you will do your part to make sure they stay happy," Devon said. He knew Deja was his daughter, but he knew Ray was going to be a big part of her life.

"I got you covered. Just keep in mind that we are family and my son will be in your life too, so we have to be men and be good fathers and treat Leila like she is the mother of our children at all times," Ray said, making it known he didn't want Devon acting up.

"I got you," he said and they shook hands.

"Well when you want to hang out and do what dads do with their kids, let me know," he said and Leila came down.

"Here you go Devon. I will get her this weekend and if you need me don't hesitate to call," she said and kissed Deja.

"We good. You take it easy Ray," he said.

"You too Devon and hold on. I got to get my sugar too, before DJ bounces. Give me a hug li'l momma," Ray said and Deja hugged him and kissed his cheek. "See you later, big girl," he said.

"See you later, gator," Deja said and grabbed her daddy's hand. "Come on daddy, let's go bye-bye," she said and Leila smiled. Ray was Ray, Devon was still daddy and she prayed that her family would be happy in the end.

"Bye sweetie pie," Leila said.

"Bye-bye, mommy," she said and she and Devon left. Deja was two and talking like she was five.

"Wow," he said, getting a plate from the cabinet.

"What?" she asked.

"Nothing beautiful let's eat," he said and kissed her on the forehead.

XXXVI

The baby was born, they were in their new home, Leila's house sold and Ray's loft had finally gone under contract. He had conducted business there 'til after Leila's house sold, then they were able to rent a space a few blocks from Leila's bookstore. He decided to start with a small gym 'til he was able to open a full sized spot. All of his faithful clients came along with his move and business was doing well due to word of mouth. It was scary for the both of them, but they did it. Devon and Ray were cool and he and Leila had a true friendship that Leila never thought would ever happen, thinking back on all the issues and problems they had, but they were closer divorced than they were when they were married.

The weather was getting cold and Leila was so grateful that they had all the major moving and hard work out of the way prior to the weather acting up. They were at Ray's loft, getting the last couple of boxes and Leila was sitting in her truck waiting for Ray to come down. She noticed a car parking across the street and she wondered why the car looked so familiar. She watched the little woman get out, walk past the front of her truck and go into Ray's building. She looked familiar and Leila wondered if she was a client that didn't know his business moved and after a couple of minutes she realized it was Katrina.

"Aw naw bitch, not today," Leila said, turning off the engine and getting out the truck. Katrina stepped in the elevator and the doors closed before Leila got in. She got off the elevator and was happy to see Ray's door cracked, but her smile turned into a look of disappointment when she pushed the door open to an empty unit. Ray was coming out of his room with the last box in his hands, he saw Katrina in a long coat and she opened it when she saw him.

"What's going on, Ray? You trying to move on me? I've tried calling and when your phone said no longer in service I had to make sure you was okay," she said, revealing the low cut sweater and tight jeans she was wearing.

"Kat, you got a lot of nerve coming over here," he said and Leila stopped at the door and listened before she went in.

"What'd you expect Ray? You never returned any of my calls and then no service on your phone, what was I supposed to do?" she asked like a dumb blonde.

"Stay away. I expected you to stay the fuck away. Look, I don't have time for you. I am on my way out. I am married and my wife would mop the floor with your ass if she knew you were here," he said, putting the box down. He wondered if Leila saw Katrina come up.

"You married that fat bitch?" she snapped.

"Leila yes, I married Leila and we have a beautiful son and you know what Katrina? We are doing so well. In fact, let me call my wife to come up. She's right downstairs," he said, reaching into his pocket, but Leila walked in.

"No baby, you don't have to call me. I'm right here," she said and Katrina almost passed out.

"Leila…, um…, hi…, I…, was…, um…, in…, the neighborhood and I um…," she stuttered.

"Save the shit, Katrina. Now, I hope this will be the last time we see your ugly ass again. The fat bitch has had it with you fucking with her man. Now, I'm not going to ever have to tell you again to stay the fuck away from my husband and if I ever have to tell your ass that again I will mop the floor with ya' boney ass, you got that?"

she said, stepping to Katrina and she almost pissed on herself. Ray had to run between them because he saw the fear in Katrina's eyes.

"Kat, you may wanna bounce," he said, holding Leila and she ran up out of there as if the building was on fire. "Damn, baby, calm down. You are a mother," he said, kissing her.

"And a jealous wife. I'm not having it with these bitches. They are going to feel the wrath of a big girl if they keep coming at my man."

"I see and I bet we will not be seeing Katrina's ass again."

"Oh, I know we won't," she said and he went to pick up the box.

"Okay Mayweather, let's go so we can get our kids," he said, talking about DJ and RJ.

"Yeah, let's get the kids. I'm in the mood for Chinese," she said and shut the door.

THE END

Hello Reader, if you've just enjoyed my first novel Now You Wanna Come Back, please post your review on Amazon.com and/or Barnes and Nobles.com.

Coming Soon!!!

Now You Wanna Come Back

Part 2

Book Club Discussion Questions

1. Do you think Devon was within his rights to be turned off?
2. Do you think Leila should have maintained her size during her marriage?
3. Do you think Devon was wrong for bringing Michelle with him to Leila's home to pick up the baby?
4. Should Leila have reacted differently to Michelle being in the car with Devon to pick up their baby?
5. Was Rayshon out of order with deciding to date Leila when he knew she was still married to Devon?
6. Do you think Rayshon was stupid to allow Katrina to spend the night on his sofa?
7. Do you think Katrina was sincere when she said she wanted Rayshon back or was she just jealous?
8. Do you think Leila was unfair with not believing Rayshon when he said nothing happened?
9. Do you think Leila should have taken Devon up on his offered when she felt that Rayshon betrayed her?
10. Do you think Leila was wrong for not telling Rayshon about her pregnancy?
11. Do you think Rayshon was too calm when he found out about the baby?

LUCK OF THE DRAW

anna black

"A story of love, deceit, and depicts the everyday woman." -AAMBC

Now Available

One

Kennedy wasn't in any kind of mood for going out that Saturday evening. She had just gotten off from a long day of work at the jewelry store and she was too exhausted to go anywhere. Since she owned the store, certain packages that came in could only be verified by her, so that day had her mentally and physically tired. She drove home telling herself, 'I can't wait to put my feet up and sip on a glass of something that will help me to relax.'

She walked in the door, leaving everything she carried into the house in the foyer, and told herself that she'd get it later. She climbed the steps to her bedroom with a smile on her face, because she finally reached her destination of peace, but her best friend Cherae was at her door within minutes, pressing her to go out with them to the club. She took off her shoes, trying to ignore Cherae as she took off her clothes and then she slipped into her comfy robe.

"Come on girl, all you need is a shower and you'll be refreshed. Teresa said she'd be here by 11:30 and that will give you plenty of time to get some rest and be ready. You work at a jewelry store Kay, not on a farm, so you can't be that tired," she whined and Kennedy knew that she was in for a battle if Teresa was there too in her ear to go out. She knew that she would be a no win situation if they were both there to beg and press. They always cornered her and talked her into going out with them, even when she really didn't want to go. The thing is; they drink more than she does and they know she'll be sober enough to drive their drunken behinds home, so she knew it wasn't them really wanting her to go, they just wanted to get their drink on.

"Okay man damn. I will go, but don't think I'm driving because after the day I just had I want to get some liquor in me and I'm not driving you drunk heifers home this time. I'm the one who's going to be in the back seat passed out, understood?"

"Yes, yes...," Cherae said with excitement.

"Now get out of here so I can rest my nerves before Ree gets here," Kennedy playfully ordered.

"No problem madam. I will let you be, but you know I'm gon' be right back up here to make sure you are getting ready and Kay can I borrow your little blue Donna Karen purse, I need it for tonight," she asked and Kennedy wanted to say no, because Cherae always borrowed her things, but she was too sweet to say no, it wasn't like she was going to need it.

"Yea, it's in the closet on the bottom rack, and when you come back up to so-call check on me, you better have me a glass of wine in your hand too," Kennedy said with a smile. Cherae was her girl, no matter what and she loved her to death. She did a lot for Cherae, and it didn't bother her one bit. She just wondered when Cherae was going to get herself together and stop being so needy. She was so dependant and Kennedy didn't understand how she settled, when she had so much opportunity to be so much better. She has no kids or excuses to hold her back from doing something with her life, because she wasn't paying Kennedy a dime to live there. Cherae just thought her looks would land her a rich man and after thirty-four years of trying to land a millionaire, she was still unlucky to accomplish that mission.

Kennedy walked into her massive walk-in closet and it didn't take long for her to find something to wear. She had so many clothes, shoes, purses and hats; she didn't have to go through a million and one channels to look fabulous. Kennedy was a plump woman, full-figured society would say, but at a size sixteen, or a fourteen on a good day, there was nothing bad anyone could say about her. She was conservative in some ways, but she knew how to turn on the sexy.

She loved going out with her girlfriends and even though she was the heavier sister she still turned heads when they went out together because she was beautiful and she knew she was gorgeous because her daddy taught her that.

She never felt more or less than beautiful, compared to her two girls Teresa and Cherae, and she knew that they had it going on too. Teresa was an averaged size woman, not fat at all Kennedy thought to herself when she'd hear her complaining about how she gained a pound or two. Teresa stood about five feet and at one hundred and thirty pounds she looked good in everything she wore because she was curvy. Her hips and butt filled her jeans to a tee, while her B cupped breast couldn't go without a padded bra. She had pretty dark skin and it was smooth and clear. Her short and sassy hair style would always receive compliments from women and men and it looked good on her round face.

As pretty as Kennedy thought Teresa was, she hardly understood how she always had man trouble. Kennedy realized after meeting and getting to know Teresa, that looks had absolutely nothing to do with getting a man, because Teresa's bright smile and gorgeous figure didn't make a man stay with her, and most of her men turned out to be crazy. Then there is Cherae, the bombshell of the trio. The head turner, the show stopper and there was not a man out there that she couldn't make head turn and jaw drop. She knew she looked good and didn't try to front like she wasn't the bomb. She was high yellow, with long straight dark hair. Her body was tight, because she worked out five days a week to maintain her size four frame.

Her eyes were hazel naturally, but most people thought they were fake. Her natural hair was long and straight, but jealous women swore her hair was weaved. Her pear shaped face was blemish free, with a little cute nose, and since she never knew who her dad was, Kennedy would sometimes joke that her daddy was of another race, because her momma was Kennedy's dark brown complexion and had a big nose. Cher was five feet six inches tall and although she was slim her body was shaped perfect with a C cupped breast size that could go easily without a bra for support and she never looked like a skinny girl in jeans.

She didn't have relationship issues, and getting a man was never one of Cher's down falls, meeting a man with a lot of money was what caused her problems. She had plenty of marriage proposals and dated numerous men, but she just didn't have it upstairs. She was just a beauty with no brains looking for a free ride.

Of Kennedy's two friends Teresa had all the good qualities that a woman could have including a sweet personality. She was always honest and tried to always be straight up with folks. She never acted like she was better than others and most of all she was fair. She was the cool head of the group and wouldn't argue with anyone over anything at anytime. She and Kennedy were close and spent more time together because they worked together. They met about six years ago when Kennedy took over one of her dad's jewelry stores.

Teresa had no experience nor did she know anything about the jewelry business, but she was the only person that Kennedy liked when she interviewed. She and Kennedy hit it off and realized that they had a lot in common except for their knowledge of diamonds, silver and gold. So after she promised Kennedy she would learn the business, Kennedy hired her and is so glad she did.

Cherae on the other hand was a different case. She and Kennedy had been friends their entire lives and for so long Kennedy has told her that she was not going to be able to live off her good looks, but Cherae being as irresistible as she thought she was had men paying her way for everything. She used men to her advantage, but got caught up on this one wealthy older gentleman that put her up in a nice condo downtown. He was married but that didn't mean a thing to Cher because he was very wealthy and as long as Cher took trips with him and filled in as his woman when he wanted a show piece on his arm, he took care of her.

That lasted a couple years 'til he found a younger superstar to cater to and he dropped her ass, and she had to move in with Kennedy. Kennedy wasn't so torn up about it, because she loves Cherae like a sister. She was an only child and she and Cherae were practically raised together, because they met in the second grade. When they graduated high school they parted, but briefly, because after the first year of college away from home, Kennedy was home sick and she went back home to attend school near her family. So she and Cherae were right back together. Once Kennedy got her Master's her daddy decided it was time for her to take over the store he ran and owned for twenty-four years and Kennedy was honored to take over and have her own store because her two cousins ran two other locations that belonged to her uncles Kendal and Keith.

They were a close knit family too and they were all wealthy and they accepted Cher as family until Cher dated her cousin Kory for a while and showed her natural simple ass. The family viewed her a little different after that, yet still respect her because she and Kennedy were so close. They were like "Two peas in a pod," Kennedy's daddy Kenneth would say and told his nephews to grin and bear her for Kennedy's sake. Kennedy knew they didn't care for her much after the break up, but she figured she messed over Kory like she does all men, because that was the norm for Cher. She warned Kory how Cher was prior, but no he just had to have her and she tried to drain his pockets. Kennedy tried to stay out of their relationship and not take sides, but they always involved her, so she was not sad when they finally broke up.

About The Author

ANNA BLACK is a native of Chicago, but now resides in Texas with her husband and daughter. *Now You Wanna Come Back* is her first published fiction novel and her second novel, *Luck of the Draw,* released April 2010. Her third novel *Who Do I Run To* is scheduled to release April 2012. She works as an author full time, mother and wife.

Your feedback is very important to her and she loves to hear from her readers so please, if you have enjoyed this novel share your review on Amazon and Barnes & Noble. If you need to contact her you can at any of the following:

www.annablack.net

www.annablackfans.com

www.delphinepublications.com

annablackreaders@ymail.com

www.facebook.com/ABlackAuthoress